Bon Voyage

VIET NAM

RYAN E. LONG

Table of Contents

Preface

"I just discovered I was sleeping with the enemy!" Ever have a friend say something like that to you? And yet, when your friend first met their lover, they would have said something like: "I just met the love of my life!"

How do we reconcile these two feelings?

Some might answer: "well, love is blind." But perhaps love isn't blind. Maybe it is infatuation that is blind. For those of you who don't know, "infatuation" is "an intense but short-lived passion or admiration for someone or something." Sometimes, "short-lived" can include a passionate eighteen yearlong marriage.

We become infatuated with pretty lies. We mostly hate ugly truths. No less than Plato the famous deli owner said: "none is more hated than he who speaks the truth." Nonetheless, sometimes ugly and notorious truths can help you prevent catastrophes in your life-- such as relationships that are civil wars in the making.

Find out more when you read *Bon Voyage Vietnam*.

Enjoy your read,

Ryan E. Long

Chapter 1

Ring Bandit

They were the most expensive wedding rings in the world. On July 13, 1969, they were stolen. I should know. The bride initially accused me of taking them.

That day in July was a surprisingly cool one in New York City. I arrived at St. Patrick's Cathedral on Fifth Avenue around 10:00 a.m. When I did, I saw a line of black Rolls Royce limos lined up. The busy juices of Fifth Avenue's sidewalk bustled with street vendors, pedestrians, and pigeons. A New York Police department special detail stood guard outside. Onlookers from the street cheered. Senators, congressmen, Hollywood producers, and business titans were among those in attendance.

My name is Mickey Egan, Jr. At the time, I was a 42-year old philosophy professor at Brooklyn College.

"Oh, Mickey, what a glorious day, isn't it," Sophia Gordon, the mother of the bride, said to me as she saw me walking into the church. Sophia clasped my wrist as she viewed the stream of people entering. She leaned over to kiss me on both cheeks, like she always did, and I obliged.

"It is surprisingly cool, Ms. Gordon, I agree," I said, "quite lucky we are."

She patted my hand with her finely manicured fingers.

"I'll see you at the reception after the wedding, darling," she let go of my wrist and then went to air kiss other guests who were arriving. Ms. Gordon, age 54 at the time, was the head of a local educational charity. It was rumored to have been unwritten by underworld types. She was connected to most of the people who were invited to the wedding.

Trailing not far behind Mrs. Gordon was her son, Otis, a 34-year-old Madison avenue advertising executive and his wife. He patted me on the shoulder as he walked into the church past me: "Who needs Broadway shows? This dog and pony show beats them all, eh Egan?" He smirked, patted me on the cheek, and then followed his mother into St. Patrick's Cathedral.

The cathedral was glorious. It had a 30 feet high ceiling, gothic walls, and stunning Tiffany looking glass panels within. As I walked, I was surrounded by the friends of the bride and groom, all of whom seemed to know each other directly or indirectly. The gruff looking usher came up to me, a bearded fellow who I could have sworn was Ernest Hemingway, and said "here is your ticket, son. Take your time."

He pointed me towards the front of the church. He softly, but firmly, nudged me towards my seat. I remember slowly walking forward, almost in a trance, as it was one of the many weddings I had gone to that sultry summer. I know that cause of all the stares and questions I got from those attendees when they found out I had never been married and wasn't in a relationship. From the gay men: "are you straight?" From the women: "oh, you don't know how to commit?" It was maddening when they tried to shove me into one of their pre-made pigeonholes. They themselves hated the boxes. Not very good marketing.

"Take your time," the Hemingway looking usher said to me, using the new four-letter word – "time." But most of those I was meeting at these weddings didn't care about fleeting time. They did care about appearance and how you looked to the outside world, not how you looked to yourself at the end of the day – or at the end of your life.

When I got to the church row where I was supposed to sit, there was a finely mustached man sitting next to the empty space. He was inspecting his fingernails.

"Excuse me, sir, is someone sitting here?" I pointed to the empty space.

"Not that I know of," he said as he wiped off the part of the bench where I was about to sit.

"Thanks," I said.

I slowly sat down. Out of the corner of my eyes, I could see that my dark wood colored skinned neighbor started twisting his thick mustache. As he did, he said to me:

"You aren't Walt Disney Mickey, but you'll do better than those crusty skinned dinosaurs over there," he said taking a peek in front at some of Blake Stimson's family. Blake was the groom.

"And you are?" I asked.

He peered back over at me. His James Brown bees nest of hair looked like it has been worked on for hours by a team of hairdressers.

"Maximilian Sanchez," he held his hand out, "but my friends call me Max."

I shook his hand.

"How did you know my name?" I asked Max.

"When I got the invite from Blake, I checked out the seating chart. I wanted to make sure I wasn't going to be sitting next to a Stimson crusty."

I smiled internally.

"A Stimson crusty?" I asked.

"Yeah, like when you get a bagel and it is black and crusty, soft on the inside, like they should be."

He peered back in front towards where the Stimson family was sitting, making sure they didn't hear him.

"How do you know Blake?"

"Been his banker few years now," Max said.

"How did you guys meet?" I asked.

"Naked bare back donkey rides down in Baja California," he said with a straight face looking towards the front of the church.

"Donkey rides?" I asked.

He looked back over at me. His smiling teeth peeked out from under his bonsai quality trimmed mustache.

"Come on, gringo," he slapped my knee in a friendly way as he chuckled, "we met at Harvard Business School," he said looking at some of the attractive females taking their seats, "but that whole Harvard scene can be like an acid trip donkey ride."

"I imagine so," I said.

"And how about you, Mickey? What piece do you play in this puzzle?"

"Ella and I are friends."

Max started messing with something in his expensive looking jacket, like he was looking for something, and then it appeared: a small silver flask. He was just making sure it was there, because he put it back.

"For sure you and Ella met at Harvard too, or was it at a fish taco club at Princeton?"

His mouth cracked a small smile.

"Nah," I said as people were starting to settle down around us, getting ready for the procession to start, "we met by accident on a train to Boston a few years go."

"Maybe it just looked like an accident," he said.

Suddenly, we heard the music start playing in the background. The whispering started dying down around us. Everybody in the church stood up.

"This has to mean that we have to be quiet," Max said, playfully brushing my left knee as his right knee nervously moved, like he had somewhere else to be.

Max and I looked to up towards the altar. We saw Blake Stimson take his place next to the priest, followed by his best man. As I understood things, normally wedding processions were begun when the mother of the bride marched down the aisle, followed by the bride and her father. But Ella told me her father died in World War II. And so, Sophia, Ella's mother, played the part of her father.

When Max and I looked to our right, there was a procession of immaculately dressed groomsmen and bridesmaids walking arm in arm.

"She's kind of hot," Max leaned over to me, whispering in my ear, as a brunette stunner walked by. I waved him away. He waved me away back.

The groomsmen and bridesmaids were followed by a little boy. I assumed he was the ring bearer because he was carrying what looked like a ring case. All of these little girls were wearing white spreading flowers all over the middle aisle. After they got to the front of the church, the little boy handed the sealed white case to Blake's best man.

"Word has it," Max whispered to me, "that those wedding rings are the most expensive of their kind in the world, made from some fancy platinum and maybe blessed by the Pope himself with some spring water from an unknown source in the Alps," he looked at me with wry eyes.

"Word has it, huh?" I whispered back.

"Word has it." He shrugged. "But I do know they were appraised as being the most expensive made to date, maybe even a world's record!" He tapped my left knee.

I ignored him.

Suddenly, Max and I peered to our right. There she was. Ella was walking with Sophia. Ella looked amazing. Her eyes were sparkling with joy, and her white gown, probably made by Valentino because that was her mother's favorite, dragged behind her. Sophia was wearing an elegant women's tuxedo with some type of chiffon tie.

"For sure that's Chanel," Max whispered over to me.

"Maybe," I said back.

Ella caught me and Max looking at her. She blew us a kiss. Sophia looked over at us, too. She winked.

"Foxy," Max said under his breath right after Sophia winked.

"Stunning," I said.

"That too," he said.

The procession slowly made their way up to the altar. When they arrived, the bearded Wild West looking priest officiating the ceremony indicated with his hands for everyone to sit down. Everyone in the church sat.

"We are here today to celebrate the holy union between Blake Stimson and Ella Gordon," the priest said. "We are here to welcome . . ."

Suddenly, I felt a nudge on my knee. It was Max's hand and it held the silver-plated flask he had earlier. The patrician looking woman sitting next to the left of Max was so focused on the front of the church that she didn't see the flask.

"Take a swig," Max whispered into my ear.

"What is it?"

"Tequila."

The whole scene brought me back to "growing up Catholic" in high school, massaging my girl-friend's hand as the priest said whatever he was saying in church. I remember being in a trance with her and not listening to anything the priest said. Instead, I daydreamed about being with her next to the ocean, her smiling as she splashed me with ocean water. But then the buzz would be ruined. One priest or another would smack me hand and would warn me to stop being "a voodoo witch-loving Satan worshipper during mass!" One time I whispered back: "but what would Jesus say?"

And then I'd get smacked again – this time much harder.

That's why I took Max's flask. He smiled. I sipped the tequila. It was smooth. It was fresh. For some reason, it made all of those smacks seem like they were worthwhile. Cause now I was sitting there drinking what was no doubt the priciest tequila that money could buy with the groom's banker.

Handing back the flask to Max, I felt warmer and calmer. The priest at the altar continued:

"Blake you have known Ella and have seen her beauty, the conflict free gold from within, the treasure that you discovered when you met her, and have only grown to see even more clearly as you have gone down the path of love, support, and family that has brought you here today," the priest said to Blake, who was staring at Ella very intently.

Max nudged my knee again with the flask. I took it and dove down below the bench like I was picking up something from the ground, where I partook in a long swig. Max was more cavalier. He'd just sip it right out in the open. But he'd dip his chin down enough so that it looked like he was itching his chin with something.

"And Ella, you have seen the splendor of Blake's inner being, his candor and reliability over the years, seeing all of his spirit, in all of its glory, without ever losing the wonder of what is next, making roller coaster rides in Coney Island seem boring, and sort of really expensive," the priest said.

11

I got up from bending down like I was picking something up. I looked back over at Max. He raised his eyebrows in surprise at what the priest said about the Coney Island roller coaster rides. I handed back the flask to him and I raised my eyebrows in return. I looked over to where Otis, Ella's older brother, was sitting. He caught my eye.

He winked and then looked back towards the front of the church.

I shrugged. The priest at the altar continued:

"Now, my children, you have come before me, in the eyes of the powers that be, those powers you can't see, who look over us, sometimes into us, and, yes, sometimes beyond us, to make a tie that will never break, sort of like when you tie your shoelaces twice, cause they are there to stay," the Siberian wolf-eyed priest said with utmost seriousness.

Max nudged my knee again. I just said "no."

"So, let us make this double shoelace tie so that your relationship is ready for the basketball game, soccer match, or, yes, even track meet of life. This tie will serve you, even when it is wet, rainy, and, of course, even when it snows, but only if you hug and drink and smile – often."

I remember Max and I looking at one other, wondering if this priest was for real. Nobody else in the church seemed to flinch, except for Otis, whose smirk could be seen from across the aisle.

Finally, the vows.

The bearded priest:

"Do you, Blake Stimson, take Ella Gordon to be her lawfully wedded husband, to have and to hold, from this day forward, for better, for worse, for richer, for poorer, in sickness and in health, until death does your part?"

"I do," Blake said as Ella livingly glared at him.

Blake then moved to get the wedding ring from his best man, who held out the wedding box for Blake to uncover. As Blake peeled the top of the box back, his eyebrows went through his forehead, he put his hands on his cheeks, and he started screaming. Ella put her hands over her mouth. Blake then stared at his best man.

He just shrugged.

"Holy shit, they gone," Max whispered to me.

"The rings?" I asked.

"No, the toupees," Max whispered back.

As we sat in the quiet St. Patrick's church, the woman behind me wearing the fox around her neck started screaming. The first rocks in a rock slide falling down the mountain. With Ella's hands still over her mouth in shock, and as Blake went to shake his

13

best man back and forth, I looked around and witnessed the avalanche.

In the front row sat Blake's mother. She grasped her pearl necklace. She started to scream, "where is that God damn ring, where is the ring, God damned ring bandit! You are in trouble! Trouble! You are in trouble! We're going to lock you up you son-of-a bitch, you son-of-a bitch!"

Her husband tried to calm her. But she shrugged him off and continued to yell.

Blake's cousins, nieces, and cousins of cousins visiting from out of town, or out of the country, began to yell in the hell that was the church that cool summer 1969 morning.

"Please, everyone, please calm down, we'll find the rings, they are here somewhere, just please calm down," said the bearded priest.

Everyone ignored him.

"Get the cops in here!" I heard a yell from a man in the back.

"Get the FBI in here!" Blake's mother yelled.

As they yelled, New York City police started filling the finely dressed church with men in blue.

Throughout the chaos, Ella Gordon, aged 26, kept her hands on her mouth. She stood on the altar in shock.

I turned to look at Sophia in the front row on the right side of the church. All I could see was her head leaning over to whisper into Otis's ear. He nodded and then got up. I suspected he was going to call in detectives. I think I was correct. Not long after he got up, a bunch of men who looked like undercover New York City police detectives wearing suits arrived.

As cops bled into the church and as women continued screaming, I remembered Ella telling me about the platinum ring. It was especially made by Cartier for her wedding. "Rare is our love," read the internal engraving, made by a calligraphy master in Rome, world famous for his artistic talents.

Unexpectedly, a steely gaze from the altar caught my eyes through the chaos in the church. They were Ella's sun-drenched blue eyes. It wasn't a friendly gaze. It wasn't a sad gaze. It was an angry gaze. When I caught it, I knew that Ella suspected me of taking the rings. Her hands were clinched as fists on her sides. She always knew I thought there was something fake about Blake. The red flags I will tell you about throughout this story explain why.

While they say love is blind, maybe they are talking about infatuation.

Maybe that's why Ella's "love" for Blake only grew stronger with each successive red flag.

15

Yet I didn't take the rings. I wasn't the ring bandit. Sitting there that day, I didn't know, as I do now, that the ring bandit was sitting there in the audience the whole time.

But Ella didn't care. She was certain I did it. As she kept staring at me through the tidal wave of drama, I didn't know what to do.

So, I shrugged. My shrug made her even more certain of my guilt. Her fists clinched even harder.

As Ella's eyes beamed down on me and as Max enjoyed the show, I nonchalantly looked outside the stained-glass window. I then saw a slew of pigeons take off from their perch on the church. I thought back to the first time I met Ella.

It was on a train ride from New York to Boston.

The date was September 13, 1967.

And it all started with Ella's horrendous screaming.

Chapter 2

The Pope's Pen

Just around noon the screaming started.

"Where is it, I've been robbed, where is it, I've been robbed! Oh my God!" I heard the woman's shrieking in the cabin next door on the train. I was sitting in my cabinet peacefully reading *The Boston Globe*.

I thought she was playing a charade with her husband or playacting in some scene with her friends. So, I ignored the first scream.

But then she screamed again.

"Thief! Where is the thief that stole from me? Wretched thief. Police! Police!" I heard the woman yell to the top of her lungs during that train ride in September of 1967.

It is then I knew something terrible must have happened. I put my newspaper down. I quickly got up, opened the door to my cabin, and went to the cabin next door. I knocked on it.

"Yes, please come in, please come in, please," the woman said from behind the door.

After I opened the door, my eyes gazed upon one of the most beautiful women I've ever seen. She was in obvious distress. Her messy long blond hair looking like it had been pulled at by a cave man. Her Louis Vuitton luggage was open. Her clothes were thrown all over. Papers were strewn throughout. She was on her knees inspecting the floor. The pillows from where she was sitting were all removed.

Her pale blue eyes looked up at me. She didn't say a word. It's like time stopped. I peered back at her from the entryway into her cabin. She finally broke the silence.

"Well if you aren't a sight for sore eyes," she said with a small smile that belied her stress. "Would you be a dear and help me look for it?"

She went back to her search.

"It?" I said, scratching my chin.

She continued looking, not looking up at me.

"Oh, oh, oh, yes, the 'it' is my pen."

I looked outside the train window. I thought perhaps this woman was off her rocker. But maybe it was the Pope's pen, given to her as a present by the Pope himself? Or perhaps it was from her fiancé? What did I know? My father had recently given me a fancy pen, and I knew I'd have been miffed had it went missing.

"Sure thing," I said.

Swiftly, I got onto my knees with her. I started looking.

"I'm sure I've been robbed," the woman said as she looked around on the floor and in the seats of her cabin, her elegant suit pants crinkled from her feverish search.

As I searched the floor, I asked:

"Why would someone take your pen?"

"To fence it," she shrugged. "I'm sure you wouldn't believe it, but it was a special ball point pen worth about $730,000.00 made by Mont Blanc," she said. Her Brooks Brothers suit jacket was lying open on where she was just sitting. I knew because I could see the label.

"A ball point pen worth $730,000?" I said out loud as I scratched my head.

"Yes, white gold-plated custom made by Mont Blanc," she said, "in collaboration with Van Cleef & Arpels."

The Mont Blanc pen sounded familiar. But I didn't think anything of it at the time. She opened up her Brooks Brothers sport coat to look one more time, suspecting it was hiding there somewhere, a mouse with its cheese in the tunnel that you can hear – but can't find.

I kept looking around for her.

"Oh, you are such a doll," her blouse opened up ever so slightly, revealing a neat pearl necklace around her neck. "What's your name?"

"Mickey," I said as I looked through her seat, "Mickey Egan, Jr."

From the corner of my eye, I could see her hold out her right hand. Trinkets were on her wrist. A snazzy-looking Cartier watch adorned her left.

"A pleasure to meet you, Mickey, my name is Ella," she paused, "Ella Gordon," she finished. I turned to look at her. She was now staring straight at me. Her lipstick was faded but her lips were wet. I felt unprepared for her.

We shook hands. The first thing I noticed was her handshake. It wasn't frail. Many people don't really shake hands. They feel their way through your hand as if they were in a pitch-black bedroom trying to find a toilet.

Our hands unlocked. Right about when I was going to ask her what was so special about the pen, other than its white gold plating, a New York City police officer came into the cabin. He was a gruff looking gunslinger of a man whose name-tag said: "Sergeant Amos." He barked:

"What's all the commotion about here? Did someone steal your roast beef sandwich mister?" Sergeant Amos stared at me. Old country store looking spectacles rested in a sketchy way on the edge of his nose, a diver about to jump off the board into the pool below.

"Or was it your tuna fish on rye, lady?" The sergeant stared over at Ella with a chuckle.

A cigarette dripped from the sergeant's lips. It looked like it had been loitering there for a few days, just dripping, not being smoked but also not paying any rent.

Another New York City police officer, last name "Hardin," came alongside Sergeant Amos. Officer Hardin was tall, lean, and had a beard. He towered over the sergeant.

"It's a special pen," officer, Ella paused to say. "It doesn't only have sentimental value, but it is extremely expensive. And your full name Sergeant Amos?"

"Sergeant Clint Amos," he nodded to Ella to acknowledge he wasn't afraid she asked for his full name. Amos then slapped officer Hardin on the shoulder and sarcastically said:

"Well, you know what they say, right partner? Don't matter the type of pen you use, it's what you write, isn't that what they say?"

"Yeah, yeah," officer Hardin said, massaging his Walt Whitman looking beard, "that's what they say, that's what they say," he nodded in slight agreement, "but if the pen done gone stolen, then you can't write squat."

"Frankly, sergeant," Ella interrupted, "I don't care what they say, and what you say, this pen was worth at least a $730,000.00, making whomever took it a felon."

The cigarette on Sergeant Amos's mouth suddenly got erect, as if it were standing attention. Backpedaling, the bushy Wild West mustached sergeant said:

"I didn't mean it that way, lady."

Amos took out his pad to write a report.

"The pen was given to me by my fiancé," Ella said.

"Who is your fiancé?" Amos asked.

"Blake Stimson," Ella answered.

While Amos wrote, Ella explained the pen's importance:

"It's very special to me. My fiancé spent a great deal of time shopping for it."

"They got no personal shoppers in New York?" Officer Hardin asked out loud as he massaged his cosmopolitan hillbilly looking beard.

"Yeah, good question, they got none of that locally, miss?" Sergeant Amos asked.

Ella stared with scorn at both police officers and their cavalier attitude towards what, in her mind, was a most serious affair.

After taking Ella's name and address Sergeant Amos asked her as he looked at me:

"This your husband?"

"Oh, him, no, he's a nice gentleman who was next door and heard me screaming." He came into to help me look for the pen."

"Yeah, well, in that case, we should take you out in the hallway then, Ms. Gordon, cause we going to ask you some personal info," Sergeant Amos said.

The two extremely strange New York City police officers exited the cabin with Ella and I kept looking in a hopeless way for her pen. After a minute or two of questions, the three came back in.

Sergeant Amos looked to me.

"What's your name, mister?"

I looked up from the floor towards the cigarette dangling from Amos's mouth, the smoke creating a screen in front of his pitch white country boy looking skin.

"Mickey Egan, Jr., officer."

I gave him my address and other contact details.

"Where was you when this here Ms. Gordon went screaming an all?" Sergeant Amos asked me, cigarette smoke heading south into my face as he peered down at me.

"I was next door, in the cabin next door," I nodded, "reading the newspaper."

"And what caused you to come into Ms. Gordon's cabin?"

"I heard her screaming," I looked over to Ella, her forehead in her hand. "I thought maybe someone was play acting a scene from Shakespeare, so I didn't come right in," I now turned to look back up at the officer, "but then she kept screaming and that's when I came over."

"Yeah, yeah," Amos said as he wrote, like he agreed with what I was saying, "and about what time was that Mr. Egan?"

At this point I got up and stood.

"I'd say it was about, let's see," I paused as officer Hardin pointed to the report and sergeant Egan nodded his head, making a change. "I'd say it was about noon."

"Roger, roger," Amos said. "So about exactly when would you say that pen went missing, Ms. Gordon?"

Ella was now sitting.

She calmly smoked a Chesterfield cigarette. I knew they were Chesterfields cause of the box sitting next to her sport coat. Closing her eyes, she said:

"I got onto the train and got myself settled. The train left from New York City about 10:00 a.m. I got my papers out and did some preparations for my talk. I was sort of fatigued, so I put everything away and went to freshen my face in the bathroom."

"About what time was that, Ms. Gordon?"

Officer Hardin just stood there, listening, with his arms crossed, as he took notes – or perhaps drew in his notepad.

"I'd say it was about 11:30 a.m.," she said.

"Yeah, and about how long was you in that toilet thing over there," the officer nodded towards the train toilet.

"Oh, it wasn't long, just a fresh splash on the face like I always do before I take a nap."

Bearded officer Hardin kept writing – or doodling -- in his pad.

"And what time you'd say you got back to this cabin for your shut eye?" Sergeant Amos asked.

"I'd say it was about 11:40."

As Amos wrote, Hardin picked at something in his mouth, inspecting it. Amos then asked:

"Where was the pen the last time you saw it, Ms. Gordon?"

"It was on the inside of my sport jacket," she nodded over to the Brooks Brothers jacket.

"You mean right there?" The raspy Amos pointed to where her wallet was stored.

"Yes," she nodded.

He took a note and I went to sit down.

"Now, let me ask you Ms. Gordon," Sergeant Egan said, "did you check your coat when you came back into your cabin to take your nap?"

"No, I just laid down and took my shoes off. Fell asleep pretty quickly."

Out of the blue, officer Hardin chimed in:

"You close the door to your cabin, did yah?"

She looked over to towering officer Hardin, whose deep blue eyes reminded me of those waters you sometimes see in Caribbean postcards:

"Yes, of course, I closed the door," she responded.

"And you first noticed it missing when?" Amos asked.

"When I woke up from my nap around noon. I went to get the pen from my sport coat. But it wasn't there."

"That's when you started screaming?"

"Yes," Ella nodded.

Sergeant Amos offered a cigarette from his box of Marlboros to us.

"No thanks," I said.

"I have my own, thanks sergeant," Ella said.

Amos shrugged. Officer Hardin helped himself to one, a free candy on Halloween. Amos paid no mind. It was like their routine. Egan lit up Hardin's cigarette, and then lit up his own. In a philosopher type of tone, Amos then looked over to Ella:

"Now, a most relevant question for our thorough analysis of this most terrible crime, Ms. Gordon."

A "most terrible crime?" Was this guy joking? I sort of smirked to myself. She didn't pick up on it.

"A most thorough analysis indeed, I'd done agree with you," said officer Hardin. Then Amos asked:

"Did anything else go missing out of your things?"

"No, sergeant, that was it," she said as Amos wrote, showing his notes to Hardin, who nodded in agreement, pointing here, pointing over there, as though they were admiring a drawing.

"Right, right, interesting," officer Hardin said as Sergeant Amos wrote. After a minute of writing, Amos closed his black book and looked up.

"I think that will be it, Ms. Gordon. We will give you a call if we find anything out," Sergeant Egan said. He shook her hand and then came to shake mine. Officer Hardin did the same.

The two officers exited the cabin.

I looked over to Ella.

"Want some chocolate? I got a little Cadbury left here," I opened up my sport coat and picked some out.

She finished her cigarette. When she looked over, a small crack of happiness was in her eyes: "Sure, Mickey, a small piece of chocolate to end a horrible day sounds about right." I put the wrapper of chocolate on my knee.

We were now sitting on the same bench in her cabin. She picked at the chocolate from the wrapper and closed her eyes as she ate. She sighed a small sense of relief. I thought I'd get her mind off things. So I asked:

"Why you going to Boston?"

She kept her eyes closed, eating the chocolate, as if she was in a sauna. She then answered:

"For a conference at Harvard Business School that I am giving on how to run a non-profit profitably."

"I thought non-profits weren't supposed to make profits?"

She reached over to grab another piece of chocolate from the wrapper without even looking.

"Yeah, well, there are other ways to measure profits, such asking questions like: how many kids are graduating high school per dollar invested, how many of them are going to college, and how many of them are getting jobs after college?"

"Got it," I said. I looked outside the window at the Boston suburbs.

She opened her eyes and looked over to me.

"And why are you heading to Boston, Mickey? Body building seminar?" She smirked as she took another piece of chocolate and peered at my tweed jacket, a hand-me-down from my pop.

"Yup," I said looking at my arms, "tenth year in a row. I've won all ten competitions except nine."

We both giggled.

"Boston Back Bay Station," the train conductor said, "15 minutes."

"Well," she said as she got up, getting her papers together and putting them into her satchel, "that was quick."

"That's what all the women say," I said as I closed the chocolate wrapper up.

She looked over at me with a twinkle in her eye.

"My fiancé and I are having a party coming up. I'd love for you to come, Mickey."

"That would be fun," I said, "what's the date?"

She got out her organizer from her satchel and started reviewing her schedule.

"Let's see," she flipped the pages with her long fingers, "that would be, ah, yes, it would be Friday, September 29th, 1967."

I paused for a moment to think of my schedule and then said:

"That should work fine. Let me take down your contact information. I'll call you when I get back into the city."

I pulled out the little Moleskin black book I had in my jacket, the one I made notes in or kept people's numbers in. Next to it I had the pen that my pop had recently given to me. I pulled that out, too. I opened the little Moleskin up and got ready to take down her info.

"What's your phone number, Ella?" I asked.

She didn't respond. She froze. She stared at my pen. I didn't say anything. I started staring at the pen, too, which was a silver colored Mont Blanc ballpoint. I looked back at her.

"Your number, Ella?" I asked again.

"Where did you get that?" She said.

"The pen?" I said.

She looked at me.

"Yes, the pen, Mickey."

I looked back down at the pen. I've never seen such attention paid to a pen before.

"Yeah, well, my pop recently gave this to me after I won a philosophy teaching award."

When I looked back up at Ella, her steely eyes were peering skeptically at me.

"When did your father give that to you?" She asked as she nodded to the pen.

"A week ago, or so," I said.

"Do you know where he got it?" She asked.

"Pop stole it from the Pope, it's the Pope's pen," I remember saying.

She stared at me, not appreciating the humor, then back at the pen.

"No idea," I shrugged. The pen was still pointing towards the paper on my Moleskin. "Why? I asked.

She peered back up at me from the pen.

"Cause that's the same exact pen that was stolen from me today, Mickey."

I looked back at the pen and then to her. I held up the pen.

31

"This thing?"

"Yea, that thing. It's the same exact pen that my fiancé Blake gave to me, the one that the police came and took the report for."

She kept staring at me in a disbelieving way.

"I don't know what to say. A mysterious coincidence?"

Ella ignored me.

"Yeah, well, take down my number cause we're about to arrive," she said with anger as she got her things together.

She gave me her number. I wrote it down. I remember her staring at me the whole time with intense suspicion. I was now suspect.

"We'll talk more about this mysterious coincidence when you come to the party, Mickey." She put quotation marks around the words "mysterious coincidence." She put on her sport jacket and held out her hand for me to shake. She didn't smile. "Thanks for coming to my aid today, I'm sure my fiancé will be appreciative of it, too."

"I'm sure he will," I said, unsure of what the hell I was saying.

We arrived at Boston Back Bay station. She grabbed her Louis Vuitton travel box and her satchel. "See you at the party, Mickey," she said as she left the cabin with an annoyed tone.

"See you at the party."

I left her cabin and went back into mine to get my things together. When I passed her cabin on the way out, I noticed a most colorful scarf, green, blue, orange, was left on the seat. I went to pick it up. I inspected it and saw it was an uncommon brand, "Hermes." I knew it had to be hers.

I knew she'd think I stole that, too.

I'd soon find out.

Chapter 3

Invisible Godfather

"**O**h, you are that train creep who stole Ms. Gordon's pen?"

The greeting above is what I expected from the secretary when I called Ella's office a few days later. I was sitting in my office at Brooklyn College and my door was closed. I stared outside watching some pigeons dance around food. I imagined the receptionist would think of me as one of those pigeons on the street: filthy and sketchy. I was scared to call.

But then I remembered something that my old man told me. He had been part of the Resistance in Paris during World War II. I know he'd seen a lot. "Always keep a sense of humor about yourself, son, especially when you got pigeon poo thrown in your face while someone tries to strangle you." I recall

34

asking: "why, cause pigeon poo is good luck?" He answered: "no, son, cause cow poo would have been a lot worse. Plus, a dark rye sense of Irish humor will keep you thinking creatively of how to escape."

He chuckled to himself.

As I sat there in my office, though, my doubting self gave way to my father's courageous but organized recklessness. I finally picked up the phone.

Ring, ring, ring, the phone went on that Tuesday morning, September 26, 1967.

"Good morning," the receptionist finally answered, "you've reached Ella Gordon's office. How may I help you?"

"Yeah, I am the guy who stole her fancy pen," I felt like saying. But my sarcastic self was quiet – for once. "Yes, good morning, may I please speak with Ms. Gordon?"

"May I ask who is calling?" The receptionist asked.

"Mickey from the train," I said.

"Mickey from where?" She asked.

"Yeah, um, so, please tell her I'm Mickey, Mickey Egan, Jr., from the train to Boston."

The receptionist paused. I got nervous. Train? Why the hell was some guy from a train calling Ella? What was she thinking? I closed my eyes and calmed my doubting self.

"Very well, just a moment, please," the receptionist said.

I sat there playing with the fancy Mont Blanc pen that my pop gave me. I waited for 10 seconds or so. I then heard Ella's voice.

"Either you were able to memorize the number, or that pen of, ah hem, yours works just fine," she said with slight sarcasm when she came onto the phone. She sounded like she was smoking a cigarette as she shuffled papers in the background.

I paused.

"Just pulling your leg, Mickey," she said with a giggle. It was a sort of kidding, sort of not so kidding giggle. I could tell she was still angry about the pen. She puffed some of her cigarette and then said: "Thanks for calling. Are you coming to the party?"

"Yes, yes I am," I said.

"Okay, we're having it at our apartment on Park Avenue, just down the street from my mom's place, this Friday, the 29th. Here is the address."

I wrote down the address in the same Moleskin that I took her number in.

"We start with cocktails around 7, so please get there sharp."

"Can I bring anything?"

She paused.

"Just that pen and your self," she said.

"I'll bring the pen, but not myself," I responded.

I could barely hear her guarded giggle.

"See you Friday," she finally said in a less cold voice than when she first got on the phone.

"Sure thing, Ella. See you Friday."

I hung up the phone. Her scarf from the train was on my lap. I sniffed it. It smelled very comforting. Just as I started smelling the scarf, closing my eyes, my cousin Hank barged into my office without knocking. He was just in time for our morning coffee. He asked something like, "getting in touch with your feminine side?"

"Yeah, you haven't yet?"

"I'm getting there, getting there," Hank looked at his watch. "I'll do it after our morning coffee," he smirked. "Shall we go?"

"Let's," I said. I got up from my seat and we went to the local coffee shop. We sat down and sipped our coffees, Hank, a former *New York Times* reporter, sitting across from me.

"So, what's up with the scarf?" Hank asked.

"Found it on a train to Boston. This lady who was sitting next to me left it."

"If she looks anything like the scarf," Hank said with a playful smile, "I bet she is a looker."

"You got that right," I raised my coffee to him. "But I think she thinks I stole her pen."

He shrugged.

"Plenty of other pens around. It's what she writes with the pen that matters."

Hank moved some lint off his old jean shirt like he cared there was lint on it.

"I don't know about that," I said. "The pen was worth something like six figures."

"That's a lot of book royalties," he loosened the collar of his jean shirt as if he was wearing a tie.

"Tell me about it," I pulled out the Mont Blanc pen that my pop gave me and held it vertical.

Hank joked:

"Are you happy to see me or are you getting excited for some other reason?"

I waved him off with my other hand.

"Funny," I handed the pen to Hank, "cause this pen that my old man gave to me is the same one that the lady got lifted that day on the train ride to Boston."

Hank inspected the pen with a playful smile.

"Looks like it's from a fancy pawn shop," he looked up at me and winked.

"Yeah, yeah," I waved him off, taking the pen back from him. "Thing is, she thinks I stole it from her that day on the train."

"Did the cops do a report on it?" He asked.

"Yeah, come to think of it, I think one the coppers was one of our Amos cousins," I said scratching my chin. "Think his name was Clint . . . Clint Amos . . . if I remember right."

Looking out the window, he waved me off like I was some off the wall conspiracy theorist.

"Amos is a common name, lad, I wouldn't read too much into it," he responded.

But I wasn't a conspiracy theorist. A lad named Jasper Amos married into my family, the Egan family, in the late 1800s. Jasper was an undercover police sergeant in San Francisco during the Wild West. So, too, were a slew of his offspring mostly out West – or at least that's what I thought. Maybe this Clint Amos New York Police sergeant wasn't related – but then again maybe he was with his country looking glasses and all.

Hank looked back at me with an almost invisible smirk.

"And her scarf, I bet you took that from her when she was sleeping," he sipped, "to support your double life as a black Irish table dancer?"

"Stop the malarkey," I said shaking my head.

"And shenanigans?" he said. "I can't. I'm a partner in Malarkey & Shenanigans," he looked at his Timex, "a limited liability partnership, needless to say."

"Well tell me this, senior partner, should I bring that scarf to her when I go to the party, or just keep it? I mean . . ."

"You are worried the lass will think you also took her scarf, right am I?" He sipped his coffee knowing he was right.

"Yeah, well, you could say that," I played with the leather elbow patch in my old man's jacket, one he gave me along with other clothes that I had custom tailored.

"I'll tell you something, Mickey," Hank said, "people will always have their impressions of you. In fact, what people believe to be true about you influences their actions more than what is actually true."

"Kind of like how the Salem witches were lied about, everybody saying they ate babies for their sacrifices and all just cause the Church wanted absolute control?" I asked out loud.

"Or how the Jews caused all of Germany's problems after World War I?" He asked.

"Two sides of the same coin that I am worried about, senior partner."

"And what I say is you meet propaganda, which is what people are conditioned to believe by repeating a lie over and over again, like you being a thief and all, with your cold hard . . ."

"I thought if I was hard I wouldn't be cold?"

He looked at his watch again.

"$500.00 an hour, mister Egan, so it is your dime."

I waved Hank off.

"Cold hard facts," he finished. "It's like the bully who comes after you with his muscles, once he gets his nose broken in the first second, he knows he got a lad who will cause him pain if he keeps going."

"Cold hard broken nose." I asked.

"Right," Hank said, "and so here you bring that scarf to the party and let her know you found it, just like you came when you heard her screaming."

I leaned over the table.

"And what if she and her fiancé don't believe me?"

"Then that's their fault," he adjusted the glasses on his nose, "if they want to keep you on their little black list, even if you were the lad who was there to help her, the one who should be on their white list, then you got to think of them as . . ."

"Sort of crazy for thinking of me this way?"

"Not sort of, lad," he started getting up, "they'd be down right mad and that means she is no good – nor her fiancé," Hank used quotations around "fiancé." He calmly sipped some of his coffee. "In that case, you run as fast as you can away from her, him, and everything they stand for on paper."

"What's great on paper isn't necessarily what's great in real life?"

"Something like that," Hank nodded, "great on paper can be awful off paper."

A few days later, on Friday, the 29th, I thought of my conversation with Hank when I got off the subway to go to Ella's party. The scarf she had left on the train was wrapped around the neck of the Oregon Pinot Noir wine bottle I had bought. I walked up to the apartment building and approached the English looking doorman.

"You are the pen and scarf thief," I pictured the properly tuxedoed man saying to me as I walked towards him. "Do you really think you are going to belong in that party up there?"

I sort of playfully slapped my face as I walked across the cross walk, getting the negative thoughts out of my head and replacing them with my walk and talk with Hank.

"I'm here for Ella Gordon's party," I said to the white-haired doorman.

"Very well, old chap," the doorman said to me, "may I ask for your name?"

"Mickey."

"You look a little big for a mouse," the doorman inspected me. I ignored him.

"Mickey Egan, Jr.," I said finally.

"Right, right," he said peaking at his guest list, "let me check."

I stood next to the elegantly dressed doorman for a minute. He flipped through the pages of the invite list.

"Is this your name here, mate?"

He turned the invite list around. I looked to the space in front of his index finger. Penciled in via sloppy men's handwriting was this:

"Dickey B. Handy."

As with the other invitees, an address was next to my name. Luckily, it was mine.

"That's me," I said.

"You are Dickey B. Handy?" He asked as he took the invite list back.

"My name is Mickey, Mickey Egan, Jr., to be exact, but whoever wrote that must have made a mistake."

"I believe it was Mr. Stimson who wrote this, if I recall correctly, sir."

He shrugged. I did, too.

"May I have your driver's license?" He asked.

"Sure."

I went into my coat pocket. I pulled out the driver's license and handed it to him. He compared the addresses.

"Right, right, old chap. I know this neighborhood. Now tell me, is there a bodega on the corner of your street?"

"Why do you ask?"

"Well," he looked around, "there are easier and easier ways to counterfeit licenses these days."

"Right, well, um, no, there is no bodega there."

"Very well, old chap," he handed me back my driver's license. "Have a great time up there, it's the penthouse floor," he said as he put the invite list on the ledge, took out a Chesterfield cigarette to light, and then let it loiter from the edge of his lip. I started walking but then something inside me made me want to stop and ask.

"And what is your name?"

He walked over to me. The cigarette just dangling there from his lips like a loose participle.

"Winston," he held out his hand, "Sir Winston Black." I shook his powerful manicured hand. As I did, he cracked a small smile. I felt like I had seen this man somewhere, sometime, in my life.

"Pleasure meeting you, Mr. Black," I said.

"The pleasure is mine," he said as the cigarette dangled up and down.

44

I left Winston and walked through the large ornate art deco doors of the building. I passed the large mirror. There was a vase full of fresh flowers. The black and white checkered floors were immaculately polished. I went into the elevator and pushed the button for "penthouse." When I got to the top floor, I exited. I heard loud laughter and music. I looked straight ahead. The large black door was slightly ajar. As I opened it, I saw through the cloud of smoke tuxedoed men and elegantly dressed women with martinis, cigarette holders, and some with monocles in their eyes.

One man stood out. He was telling a joke to a circle of men and women. I heard him say something like:

"So, I told the old chap when I was at Harvard, sometimes you don't need to study when you know the answers already, you know?"

They all laughed. One of the men leaned over to a woman, and I heard him say:

"Right, right, he's so right, why would you study if you know it all?"

Suddenly, I heard from my left-hand side:

"Can I take your coat, sir?"

I peered over. The skeleton skinny teen with Asiatic eyes in Ella and Blake's massive closet was standing at the ready. His name tag said: "Wu." His thin but sturdy hands looked like they had pulled many ropes on boats in the rain. While his hands were ready to take my coat, his blond-black hippy stoner hair was ready for the beach.

"Sure," I said as I handed him my raincoat. "Thank you."

"No sweat," he said as he took the coat. His tightly chiseled black olive eyes looked me over.

I felt a hand. It was on my right forearm. It was a woman's hand.

"So you decided to come," the woman's voice said.

I looked over. It was Ella. She wore a guarded smile on her face.

"What else was I going to do on Friday night?" I said with a smirk. I handed her the bottle of Pinot Noir with her scarf around it.

Ella's guarded smile turned ever more guarded.

"Where on earth did you get this?" She inspected the scarf.

"Yeah, well, I bought it from the wine shop down the street from my apartment."

She stared at me with her baby blues.

"You know exactly what I mean." She said.

"Yeah, well, you left that scarf on the train," I said peering at the Hermes scarf. "I found it on the floor in your cabin."

She stared at me skeptically for a few seconds.

"Alright, well," she looked at the wine uncertainly and almost sadly, "come in and meet my friends." She looked back up at me and took my forearm.

We walked through a slew of guests. They had names like Burt, Biff, Betty, Blair, and others that you'd find in some of the eating clubs of schools like Princeton and others. They were kissing cousins of one another. Different names, different families, but all with the same blueprint simmering underneath.

"Did he bring the pizza?" The same tall blond-haired Arian youth looking man who was telling the joke when I came in leaned over to Ella. He whispered into her ear as we walked by him.

"No, silly," Ella said to him, "this is Mickey, the guy I told you about who helped me on the train."

"Oh, yes, I thought his name was Dickey," said the man, who leaned over and offered me his hand, "pleased to meet you, name is Blake, Blake Stimson."

I held out my puny hand to shake his giant one. He reminded me of one of the statutes at Mount Rushmore. Sturdy, cold, made out of granite. I was more like one of those puppets you might see during a medieval show.

"Thanks for having me, Blake." I said uncertainly.

"Any friend of Ella's is a friend of mine," he said as he leaned over to kiss her on her check. She looked at me throughout. When I saw them together, I thought of the mechanics of a finely tuned Swiss watch. They all look the same. They work perfectly. I also thought of how I used to count sheep when I was kid, all of the sheep resembling the next. The ground hog day counting calmed me before I'd go to sleep.

"Oh, Ella, come over here, come over here, Bret is telling one of his jokes," a pearled necklace friend of Ella's said.

"Go, go," Blake said to Ella. They kissed on the lips.

"Come on, Mickey, let's go see the circus act," she took my forearm. As she did, I looked back at Blake. He was inspecting me with skeptical mistrusting eyes.

I spent the rest of the night meeting Ella's friends. I could tell part of her was happy to have me there. I was a breath of fresh air from the outside of her bubble. I felt like a break in case of emergency fire extinguisher. And yet the other part of her seemed to resent me for being there. Maybe it's cause she resented herself for being happy I was there.

"It's getting late," I leaned over and said to her after a few hours of "darlings," "old boys," and other phrases that I heard throughout the night. "I better start heading home." She stopped speaking to her friends to lean back over to me.

"Oh, do please come to our summer party at the Hamptons next year. Will you?"

She peered at me.

"Yes, it will be my pleasure."

"Okay, good," she looked around like she was selling me illegal drugs or contraband on a Canal Street night. "Do give a call to my office to get the details."

She did an air kiss on my cheeks and I returned the gesture. I started walking out of the large ornate apartment. I could sense eyes on the back of my head. I turned around and saw Blake's cold eyes looking at me as he spoke to other party goers. I ignored him.

"Had enough?" The coat rack teenager asked me, as if I was leaving a torture chamber.

"Yeah," I held out a five-dollar bill to tip him. He handed me my coat.

"Can't take tips, mister."

"Take it," I said.

"Don't have to twist my arm," the teenager said taking the money. He flashed his stained tobacco

teeth and whatever else the Louisiana swamp looking mouth had in it. I smirked back at him. I went
downstairs. The mysterious Winston Black was not
in front of the apartment building any longer.

I shrugged.

A few days later, I went to get my weekly hair-
cut at *Monday's*, a barbershop owned by Lev Hyman, in Greenwich Village. Any day, you could go
into Lev's shop and find Wall Street bankers, plumb-
ers, cops, and uptown Harlem men wearing spats
on their shoes.

"Well look who the cat dragged in," said Lev in
his custom-made suit from Rome.

"Doesn't need to be much of a cat," I said looking at my tweed coat and lean arms underneath.

"I didn't say he'd need to be," Lev said patting
the chair. I had an appointment at 12:00. So, Lev was
ready for me. I put my satchel down on the chair next
to the wall. I sat down on Lev's chair. He wrapped a
cape around me.

"So what's new in Mickey's world?" He asked,
hair parted neatly down the middle, three-piece
suit, pocket watch dangling.

"A woman, but she's trouble," I said as I opened
up that day's copy of *The New York Times*.

"Aren't they all?" He asked as he took a long
lock of my thick black Irish hair to cut.

"I don't think so." I shrugged.

"Yeah, yeah," he said. I was unsure if he agreed or disagreed.

The ambiguity was probably engrained in him. He came from a long line of Russian-Jewish criminal defense lawyers who represented the country's main organized crime figures in Los Angeles, San Francisco, Cleveland, Chicago, and New York City. Part of his blood make up was "ambiguous."

"So who is she?" Lev asked.

I turned the page of the newspaper. The headline read:

Invisible Godfather of New York: Who Is He?

"A lass I met on the train. Name Ella Gordon. She got her special pen stolen, a present from her fiancé," I said as I started to read the article, "and so I tried to help her."

Lev shrugged and said nonchalantly.

"Maybe someone didn't like her fiancé?"

I paused. I looked into the mirror.

"What makes you say that?"

"What makes me say that?" He paused as his squinty chess player eyes peered at me through his petit head. "Some say love is blind, kid," he then started cutting my hair again, "but I don't think that's so. I think that infatuation is blind."

I nodded and then started reading the article again as I said:

"I could see that. I met Ella's fiancé and I felt like they were two sheep in a long line of sheep that would put me to sleep."

"Hey, at least they calm you, kind of like herbal tea, eh?"

I nodded. I read the following paragraph in *The New York Times*:

> *According to one confidential source, the "Invisible Godfather of New York" is appointed for four-year terms, as with the president. A Commission that meets every year in Chicago elects him. The source, who calls himself Strawberry Shortcake, says "yeah, this guy doesn't say nothing to nobody, cause all of his orders come through newspaper crossword puzzles. And nobody knows anything about what this guy writes in the crosswords except for the one cat in the city that has the key. And this Godfather's orders come in the most stupid answers, so if the answer is 'bird' he'll put 'turd.' We asked Strawberry Shortcake what that means. "How the hell do I know? I just follow the orders."*

I looked back in the mirror at Lev. I asked:

"Ever hear of this Invisible Godfather of New York?"

"Heard of him, but never seen him, kid," Lev said straight faced in the mirror.

"Yeah, yeah, very funny," I said.

"Going to see this Ella broad again?" He asked.

"Yeah," I said as I flipped through the pages of the paper. "Going to a party they are having in the Hamptons next summer."

He patted me on the shoulder.

"Well, my only advice is this, kid, cause I known your pop for a while and I think he'd approve. Some broads like this Ella are turned on by paper, what's on paper, so that they lose sight of what's not on paper," he kept cutting. "The paper distracts them from real time."

I flipped the page of the newspaper.

"So what does that mean?"

"It means, kid," he started finishing up my hair cut, "it's like the tail of appearance wagging the dog of reality. So enjoy the sites at the Hamptons zoo but don't touch the zoo animals while they are in their cages." He wiped the hair off my shoulders and took my cape off. "How does that look?"

I looked into the mirror. As I did, a Wild West mustached guy who looked Sergeant Amos from the train came into Lev's. I looked over through the cigarette smoke to the people sitting on the long couches waiting to get haircuts. One peeked over his *Wall Street Journal* newspaper. His Asiatic black olive colored eyes resembled those of the teen in Ella and Blake's closet. Lev took me out of my thoughts:

"What are you, Miss Universe looking into the mirror that long?"

He patted me on the shoulder.

"Sorry, Lev, looks great," I said as I got up. "But what about when the Hamptons animals are out of their cages?" I asked looking at him.

"Hey," he wiped some hair off my face, "then you go on safari with them." He smiled as I handed him some cash.

"See you next time," I said as the next customer came to sit on the chair.

"See you next time, kid," Lev said.

As I walked past Lev's, I saw a *New York Times* crossword puzzle sitting on the adjacent chair. It was neatly filled out in neat all caps handwriting. I peeked closer and saw written in one of the answers: "turd." I looked back at Lev as he spoke to the Wild West mustached man who looked like Sergeant Amos from the train.

I asked myself: is Lev the Invisible Godfather of New York? Is he the one who stole Ella's pen? The one who left her scarf on the train floor?

My attendance at Ella's Hamptons party in the summer of 1968 would bring me closer to the answer.

Chapter 4

"Therapist" Girl

"Get him out of here! Get that trash out of here! Who let him in?"

When I arrived at the entrance of the brightly lit tent on the Gordon compound overlooking the Atlantic Ocean in the summer of 1968, I pictured the attendees thinking this. Maybe it was me. But everyone at the Hamptons party seemed to know one another when I peered inside the tent, Louis Armstrong's jazz band playing "Wolverine Blues."

"Your name, sir?" Winston, the same doorman from their Manhattan apartment, asked dryly.

"Yeah, um . . ." I scratched my head. "My name is . . ."

Winston held out the guest list. He pointed to my name. It was written with a pencil: "Dickey B.

Handy." With the guest list staring me in the face, Winston asked wryly:

"Your alter ego, perhaps?"

"No, but someone keeps misspelling my name," I said down to the shorter Winston. I then looked behind me. I spotted a shadow underneath a large tree. I looked over at another tree farther in the distance. Another shadow was there. I presumed the shadows were a security detail.

"Right, right," I heard Winston say. When I looked back down at the shorter butler cum door-man, he had pulled the guest list back in front of him. With his Chesterfield cigarette waiting like an eager date on his lips, he wrote on the list as he said: "I'll have a word with Mr. Stimson about his penmanship."

"I don't think it is his penmanship," I responded with frustration in my voice.

What had I done to Blake Stimson to make him resent me so? Maybe he knew that I knew what was underneath his window dressing? Over the sounds of the jazz band playing, I heard a tree branch fall in the background. I looked over. Cigarette smoke was coming from behind the tree.

"Maybe it's Blake's martini mix," Winston said. I looked back over at him. He had put what appeared to be a nice-looking pen back into his coat pocket. I know because I saw the pen's tip.

"Maybe," I said down to the white-haired man. I started to get my driver's license from my coat pocket.

Winston held up his right hand. A cloud of smoke surrounded his head.

"No need, Mr. Egan," he said, "we've already spoken about the bodega on your street."

Taking my hand out of my jacket: "but there is no bodega on my street."

He flashed a knowing smirk back at me.

"Have fun with the mummies," he said as he lifted the red velvet rope to the tent.

I shrugged. I slowly walked into the tent.

Sarcastic Winston wasn't kidding. Among the guests at Ella and Blake's summer Hamptons party were many women and men with ashy mummy white skin. Their clothes were immaculate. Some looked at me. Ever so briefly, I could see their internal radar take my reading. And then, once they knew I wasn't someone of importance, I became a flock of seagulls they ignore – or maybe resent -- at the beach.

Like pepper sprinkled among salt were the younger party guests. In their 20s, 30s, and 40s, these female souls smoked mostly from their cigarette holders. Their boyfriends were constantly pulling out their Victorian looking cigarette cases to offer one of their "old chaps" another cigarette. I knew they used "old chap" because I could hear it repeated over and over again as I went to the bar.

"Watch you having?" Asked the boxer looking bartender. A name plate like you'd see on a New York City police officer was on his black vest. "T. Vivaldi" it read.

"Gin and tonic please," I asked.

I then peered over all of the attendees in the smoke-filled tent. A long table was in the middle filled with fish, steak, shrimp cocktails, and other elegant looking foods. Long candles burnt brightly. The moon soaked Atlantic-ocean was in the distance. A breeze came and washed my face with salt water smelling air. I closed my eyes.

"Yeah, here you go pal," Vivaldi the bartender said.

Opening my eyes, I looked back over at the thick handed Vivaldi.

"Thank you," I picked up the drink and raised it to him. I took a long sip. I placed it back down on the mahogany bar. I put my hand into my linen jacket. I pulled out my wallet and started to grab some cash.

"Can't take it, pal," Vivaldi held his hand out.

I shrugged and put the wallet back.

"Then how about at least a joke?"

"Yeah," he dried a glass, "I can take that." He nodded. Sweat drips were spread all along his forehead, his slicked back hair looking olive oil filled, his tuxedoed hillbilly beard dripping down on his crisp white shirt.

"Hear about the new Japanese-Jewish restaurant in The Bronx?"

"Latkes & Sushi Inc." He answered.

"Close," I said and sipped my drink. "It's called So-Sue-Me."

"Yeah, I have to go there on my day off, pal. Sounds like my kind of place," he chuckled.

"Tony, is he bothering you?" I heard a woman's voice from the background say. Now I knew what the "T" meant in his Vivaldi name plate.

"Yeah, a doggy wouldn't wear his cologne," Tony the bartender said.

I looked behind me. Ella was standing there.

"Well, hello there, stranger," she said.

She leaned over for me to kiss her cheeks. I complied. She smelled of lemons and green tea. She wore a long flowing white linen dress that went down to her ankles.

"Dickey Handy at your service," I said as I kissed her cheeks.

"Is that your stage name?" She asked as she pointed to my drink and held her index finger up to Tony. A belt was wrapped around her waist to keep her dress all together. Her fresh smelling bare chest was yelling at me.

"Coming right up," Vivaldi said to Ella.

"Yeah, you know, a man has to make his ends meet somehow these days," I shrugged and looked around.

Some of what seemed like Blake's friends walked by, exchanging kisses with her on her cheeks just like I did.

"Your drink, Ella," Tony the bartender said.

"Oh, you are a doll Tony," she said.

Ella picked up the drink and held it up to me.

"I'm glad you came," she said.

"Me too," I said with a mischievous smirk on my face. She cocked her head and returned my playfulness with her lips.

We clicked our glasses and sipped our gin and tonics.

"Shall we take a tour?" She nodded to the crowd in the distance.

"Let's," I nodded.

I looked back at Tony.

"Thanks for the laugh," I raised my drink to him.

"Yeah, let me know where to send the bill."

He winked at me.

As Ella and I walked through the jungle of people smoking, drinking, laughing, dancing, and eating, we spoke. With Mr. Armstrong's music blaring in the background, we had to lean over to talk in each other's ears.

"Most of these people I can't stand," she said to me while smiling at some of the older mummies who were staring at her.

"Then why do you have them here?" I asked.

"Mostly friends of Blake's family," she shrugged, "only a handful of my family's friends are here," she looked around, "but they are probably out under the trees."

I looked at her.

"Doing what?"

She shrugged.

"Playing craps," she took a sip of her drink, "or if it's my older brother Otis," she raised her glass to a young couple, "he's probably French kissing his fiancé."

I looked around. I leaned over to her. I whispered to her:

"Making out behind the tree?"

She looked back over at me.

"Or something more," she said shaking her head in disapproval. "He's one of those Madison Avenue types," she took another sip of her drink. "They found him once around five in the morning sleeping on the A train uptown after a long night, new ad copy written on his little pad that eventually won the client over," she shook her head again. "He was presumed missing in action before cops found him."

"Yeah," I said looking up at the white tent, "I bet they found him with a big ole Cheshire cat grin when they finally caught up with him."

Ella looked at me with surprise as she tapped my shoulder.

"How did you know?"

"Fits the character profile. The 'random madman' who isn't random and isn't mad."

"Shall we?" She pointed to an empty table. The ocean was not far in the distance.

"That's My Desire," a song by Armstrong that was sung by him and Velma Middleton, came on.

"Let's," I nodded to the table.

We sat next to one another. Nobody else was at the table. We peered over across the other side of the tent. There was Blake. He was the center of attention at another table. His bright perfect teeth shined. Self-satisfied that everyone at the table hung on all of his words, he was oblivious that his wife-to-be was staring at him. I could tell Ella was hurting on the inside, perhaps because I had that rare witch – otherwise known as a wizard – in my blood that night.

I tapped Ella on her shoulder with the back of my hand.

"Did I tell you about my Wall Street friend who quit and started a band?"

Her trance was temporarily broken. She looked over at me with a small smile. A little sun peaking-out on otherwise overcast day.

"Do tell," she said as she sipped her drink.

"Yeah, well," I looked around and crossed my legs, like I was making a presentation to a jury or a board. "He was one of the most successful investment bankers in Wall Street history. He'd smell quality roses when other people only smelled filthy manure."

"Maybe he was just crazy," she said sipping her drink.

"People like Copernicus are often thought of as crazy when, in fact, it is the people around them who are."

In case you didn't know, Copernicus was the one who said the Earth wasn't the center of the universe. Meanwhile, those around him called him a crazy heretic.

"Fair point, my son, fair point," Ella said, loosening up as she sipped.

"So this guy shorts the market on all types of things, you name it, and makes a mint, and then, one day, when he hears a Rolling Stones song, decides to quit."

"You mean he decided to quit in the future, like later?" She asked.

"Nah," I adjusted my pants like I cared if they were drooping as I sat. "He literally quit that day, and, to make up for it, he let the bank keep his severance money."

"Sounds flakey," she shook her head.

I waved her off.

"Not for all the money he made that bank and their clients," I sipped some more. "Plus, he agreed to play an advisory role but only on one condition."

She played with the straw in her drink and asked:

"What was that?"

"They'd need to hire him and his band at least once for one of their Christmas parties."

She looked over at me.

"You can't be serious," she said with disbelief.

"Oh, yea, he had been in a band for some time, playing in basement parties all throughout New York City, but nobody every knew."

A slew of what I figured were Blake's friends walked by. They peered at us as would a Gestapo detail. Ella and I raised our glasses to them. They raised their glasses to us. Ella leaned over to me and whispered.

"So why did your friend really quit and go into music?"

I whispered back:

"So he could grow his hair out and have more fun with women," I said.

"That's what I thought," she said with a satisfied smile.

We did a cheers with one another.

"But, in his defense, he did get to do more charity work, started giving guitar and surf lessons to kids in the city," I said.

"You mean couch surfing lessons," she said as she looked at her empty glass, playing with the ice.

"Those too," I agreed.

She almost spit out the remaining gin and tonic in her mouth.

I patted her on the back.

"Can't be that bad," I said in jest about the drink.

She shook her head.

"No, it's just that your friend, what's his name?"

"Dakota," I said.

"Yeah, well, he sounds like my older brother."

"Want another drink?" I asked.

She held up her empty glass and shook it.

"Coming right up," I said.

As I got up, she pulled her clutch out. A pack of Chesterfield cigarettes made their appearance. I thought maybe Winston the butler got her into those. I shrugged.

"Two more, please," I said to Tony when I got to the bar.

"Don't you have enough kids, pal?" He said finishing his cigarette, rolling down his sleeves to cover the tattoos that were on his sailor forearms.

"Nah, I need two more bunk beds to make the room feel complete," I responded.

"Suit yourself," Tony shrugged, pushing his cigarette into the grass.

As he started making the drinks, I asked him:

"Do you know who Otis Gordon is?"

"Do you know what Hershey's Chocolate is?" He shot back.

"Right, yeah, um," I played with some grass next to my white buck shoes, "is he in here?"

Tony shrugged.

"Usually he doesn't like these parties."

"You mean his sister's parties?"

Tony stopped making the drink. He just stared at me. I think I caught his drift. I then asked:

"Right, well, um, do you see him in here."

As Tony started pouring some more gin into one of the glasses, he looked around.

"Yeah, Otis is over there."

Vivaldi finished making one of the drinks.

"Where over there?" I looked behind me.

"Over there," Vivaldi nodded his head, "that nerdy looking guy with the glasses."

I looked more closely. I saw a man of about 33 years of age. He wore a white Irish linen shirt, black knit tie, white linen suit jacket, and black linen pants. He wore black espadrilles – those slip-on shoes they wear in places like Marseille. One shoe looked like it was about to slip off. His hair was perfectly part-ed on the left. But his hair was otherwise messy. It was like he had been tussling around on the grass. He wore black rounded glasses. I imagined many a librarian has worn them. His eyes were closed. He had a cigarette dropping from his mouth. His head was resting softly on a woman's shoulder. She was much taller than him and was petting his head. He may have been unconscious. But I couldn't tell. His arms were interlaced around her for support.

I asked Tony:

"That guy, the one who looks passed out? That's Otis Gordon?"

Tony looked.

"Yeah, that guy."

Tony went back to making the second gin-and-tonic.

"That's Ella's older brother?"

"Yeah," Tony said.

I couldn't believe it. How could a man who looked like that be related to a woman who looked like Ella? Did they have different fathers? Or maybe different mothers. Otis had a slight look to him as though he never grew beyond boyhood. Ella was clearly on her way to being a full-fledged woman.

"Unbelievable," I said to myself under my breath, still staring at Otis, whose only movement other than moving his feet was to intermittently pick the cigarette in-and-out of his mouth, like you'd see an oil rig do. An old man's smirk was plastered on his mouth.

"They say truth is weirder than fiction for a reason, pal," Tony said as he put the two drinks on the bar.

"Yeah, well maybe they know what they are talking about," I nodded to Tony.

He winked slightly. He went back to preparing more drinks behind the bar. I walked slowly back to Ella, who was finishing her cigarette. She put the ash into a black oyster ashtray that was on the table.

"Here you go," I said. I slowly started putting the drink next to her.

"Merci," she said. "Where do I put the tip?"

I opened my jacket. I loosened my pants around my waste as a male stripper would.

"This could work," I said playfully.

"Yeah, yeah," she said, "let's see the goods first," she said looking at the drink. I finished placing it on the table.

I sat down. I started mixing my gin and tonic with the straw that Tony put in the glass.

"Cheers," she said.

"Cheers, lass," I said.

We clicked glasses and sipped our drinks.

"I think I caught a glimpse of your brother," I said as I played with the ice.

"Oh, yeah, was he rolling naked in the mud?" She broke a loving smirk.

"Nah," I shook my head, "he was dancing on the floor."

"With himself?" She sipped more.

"No, with some exotic Brazilian-German looking woman with beautiful hair."

She shrugged.

"Must have been a mannequin," Ella said.

"I didn't know mannequins can dance."

"New ones can. They are from Cal Tech in California," she said as she smirked.

"Why doesn't Otis like coming to these parties?" I asked.

Ella looked at me with surprise.

"Who told you that?"

"A little birdy," I said and sipped my drink.

"I didn't know birds who are retired boxers could talk," she peered back over the scene on the dance floor.

There was a pause between us. She pulled out another Chesterfield cigarette. I had a Zippo in my jacket. I pulled it out and lit her up.

"Thank you," she said.

She puffed. She then confided:

"He doesn't like Otis."

"Who? Jesus?"

"Nah, I think Jesus gets a guilty kick out of Otis. I mean Blake."

"Why doesn't Blake like Otis?" I asked.

Ella shrugged. She puffed her cigarette. Slowly the smoke came out.

"Blake thinks Otis is an oddball, an unserious person, someone who's a clown, doesn't take anything seriously."

"So what?"

Ella looked at me.

"You don't seem to know Blake. He is a serious man. He comes from a serious family. Harvard Business School, Choate boarding school, types like that don't like those who they consider to be free spirits."

I played with my drink.

"Maybe some free spirits have a method to their madness."

"It doesn't matter," she said smoking. "Old boys like Otis don't mix with manly men like Blake. They are like oil and water."

"Yeah, maybe," I said, "but who is the water and who is the oil?"

Something told me that Blake controlled her environment with his own propaganda. Anything that challenged the impression that he wanted to give her would be strangled. But I didn't get the impression, for some reason, that Otis could be strangled. He seemed too eccentric and unpredictable to be strangled – unless it was a kinky strangle.

I looked at Ella. She ignored my question. She just played with her drink. Just then, I realized why they say "speaking of the devil" when someone shows up you were just talking about.

"Well, is this girl and boy scout coffee talk?" Blake said as he pulled his jacket off. He placed it on the chair. He then sat down next to Ella. A cool breeze came in from the ocean. As they kissed, I looked out onto the incoming waves.

But I felt her long hair rub on my arm. It's like Ella was connecting with Blake physically, but metaphysically with me. I saw her blond streaks rub all along my right arm. Suddenly, I saw through the corner of my eye a white piece of paper on the grass below.

I leaned down.

Written on it in the same handwriting as I saw on the guest list:

"Therapist girl: 212.925.9123."

I could hear that Ella finished kissing Blake. I think she caught me looking down. That's cause her hand reached down. It grabbed the piece of paper. I looked up at her. She stared at the paper.

She then looked at me with angry sad eyes.

"Drop this?" She turned around and said to Blake, who was speaking to one of his Harvard Business School buds.

Blake turned around. Full of hubris, he looked at Ella, expecting another kiss. But his eyebrows raised in surprise as he saw his therapist girl hand writing on the piece of paper. It's like he just got a cancer diagnosis that he never expected.

"What's that?" He asked like he didn't know.

"It fell out of your jacket," Ella responded.

Blake took the piece of paper. He leaned over to whisper to Ella. She leaned over to listen. Nobody else could hear. But I could roughly hear what they said.

"She's a therapist of mine, been stressed lately," he whispered. He leaned back out. He placed the paper back in his inner coat pocket. "I don't know you got out," he whispered to the piece of paper like it disobeyed him, "you were paper clipped right inside my inner rain coat pocket when I gave it to the coat check boy." Blake leaned back over to whisper to Ella: "my therapist is a psychologist, went to Harvard."

Ella leaned away from him. She took a long sip of her drink. She just sat there as Blake went back to speaking to his friend. I could tell the night would be awkward from then on out.

"I had better get the last train to the city," I leaned over and said to Ella.

As she played with her drink, she said:

"I understand."

She sadly patted my hand on the table. I went to say goodbye to Blake. He shook my hand. He didn't even look at me.

As I left the tent, I passed by "Wu," the coat rack boy who I also saw at Ella and Blake's party in Manhattan. There were a number of umbrellas and rain coats in his closet. One never knows what a Hamptons summer will bring. As I passed by, I saw a paper clip on the table. I didn't think anything of it. I thought maybe it was left there by someone.

But then I saw the coat rack boy's eyes.

Those Asiatic black olive eyes I couldn't forget.

A cigarette dangled from the teen's lips.

As he handed a couple their items, he caught a glimpse of me.

The boy grinned. His tobacco stained teeth said it all.

Chapter 5

In Hindsight, A Cliff

A few weeks later after their Hamptons summer party, I checked my mail and opened up a fancy envelope from Blake and Ella. A paper clip fell out. An invitation inside read:

The Future Mr. and Mrs. Stimson
Engagement party
At the Carlyle Hotel
New York City
Saturday, October 12, 1968
7:00 p.m. – 9:00 p.m.
RSVP Required

I looked down on the floor. I picked up the paper clip from my apartment building's black and white checkered floor. I inspected it. I quietly said to myself:

"Odd. I wonder if this is the one that Blake had in his coat?" I inspected it further. I thought to myself: it looks like the paper clip that Wu the coat check teen had in front of him at the Hamptons Party.

I looked outside. But my thoughts were interrupted.

Ring, ring, ring, ring!

I could hear the phone ring in my apartment. I took the invite and the paper clip. I ran up to my apartment. I rushed in. With an out of breath voice, I picked up the phone.

"Hello, hello?" I asked over the phone. Lev the fancy barber then said:

"Yeah, so, is you going to send Frankie to get a cut instead?"

Frankie was my mini Australian shepherd dog.

"Yeah, she's on her way," I said.

"Come on, we waiting." Lev hung up.

I looked at my watch. I just realized I had a hair appointment that day. I suppose I got caught up having coffee with Ella. I'd been having quite a bit of them lately with her. Like a dump truck, she unloaded all of her anxieties on me about the coming wedding: whether Blake's parents would like the designs she picked out, if Blake would like the seating arrangements, and whether he'd like her friends. She'd usually say all of this looking out the window, not seeing herself as I saw her. She was so consumed by the four corners of Blake's resume that she didn't seem to look beyond it. Suddenly, Lev's comment to me once shot into my consciousness: "What if the stock prospectus is puffed?"

"Shit," I said out loud. Frankie was sitting on the couch. Her head was resting softly on her little feet. She had seen this scene before. I was often late for Lev's appointments. I waved Frankie off. She ignored me, too. I quickly got my satchel and left the apartment to walk over to Lev's, which was about a ten-minute walk from where I lived in Greenwich Village. On my way there, I heard:

"Mickey, Mickey, try," said the dumpling woman on my corner as I walked by.

"Xiexie," I said, which means "thank you" in Chinese. I grabbed one and put it in my satchel.

Down the street, I got:

"Don't you want to try no Coney Island dog, Mickey? Got fresh ones today pal," said Tony's "cousin," Vincenzo, as he held up a Nathan's dog in a bun.

"I'll pay you later," I said as I grabbed the dog, put it in a bag, and then shoved it in my satchel.

Vincenzo waved me off. He took a bite of one of his dogs, enjoying it, his hand resting on his belly.

A few minutes later, I arrived at Monday's.

Lev was sitting on his chair reading *The Wall Street Journal*. Cigar and cigarette smoke filled the barber shop. A cacophony of suits, jeans, suspenders, overalls, fedoras, and Yankee hats could be seen.

Sort of out of breath, I said:

"Sorry for being late, Lev," I wiped some of the sweat from my forehead. A slew of men were waiting for their cuts and chatting among one another – some manicured with pinky rings, others with rough dirty hands, still others with accountant looking fingers. Whomever says women gossip up a storm at their hair salons have never seen a place like Lev's.

"Put my munchies on the file cabinet," Lev said without looking up at me. So I took his foodies out of my satchel and placed them on top of his wooden file cabinet, which he used for "customer outreach," he said.

He slowly got up out of his chair, folded *The Wall Street Journal*, and put it on the chair next to him. The chair always seemed to be vacant. He started sharpening the razor. I took off my seersucker jacket and hung it. I peered in the back of the shop, where men got massages. A stunning Japanese woman wearing lipstick promptly closed the fancy looking drape. I shrugged. I went to sit down on Lev's seat. I picked up *The New York Times* that was hanging on a bamboo stick on the way there.

"How's the love life, sonny?" Lev asked as he started prepping me for his operation, putting his fancy Louis Vuitton branded cape around me – but instead of it saying "Louis Vuitton," it said "Monday's," but with the same font.

"Too tired to talk about it," I said as I peered at the front page of *The New York Times*, the headline for which read something like:

February's Tet Offensive Deaths: Up From Initial Estimate

"Yeah, I bet your right hand is fighting with your left on who gets the next date," Lev started taking my hair into his hand to cut.

"I've told them to get therapy," I retorted, "they got to learn how to share."

"Yeah, yeah, how is that broad you told me about?" He stopped to light up his Chesterfield cigarette.

"Oh, yeah, Ella, I feel like her therapist."

He took a long puff and let the smoke out. His chess player beady blue eyes looked at me in the mirror. He smirked. With the cigarette dangling from the corner of his mouth, he said:

"Maybe this Ella should go and see the same shrink your two hands is seeing, huh?"

"Yeah, well, then the shrink would have a conflict."

He pointed his comb at me in the mirror.

"You got a point there, counselor." He kept cutting.

"I don't know," I said, "they say love is blind, but maybe infatuation is."

Lev was quiet as he cut. I continued to read the Tet Offensive article. According to my pop's retired spy friends from World War II, much of what was reported about the Vietnam war – including the Tet Offensive -- was unreliable. Pop met these colorful characters -- American, Russian, and English spooks – during his time in Paris.

Many of these men believed the war was a catch-22. Their beliefs were not unfounded. I remember a quote from President Eisenhower: "I cannot conceive of a greater tragedy for America than to get heavily involved now in an all-out war in any of those regions, particularly with large units." Another from President Kennedy: "Communism cannot be met effectively with the force of arms. It is the peoples themselves that must be led to reject it, and is to those peoples that our policies must be direct-ed." My pop's retired spook friends also thought the Vietnam war's escalation could had been prevented by negotiating directly with "Daddy War Bucks," meaning the financiers of the Viet Cong in Moscow and Beijing.

Lev suddenly interrupted my thoughts:

"Love isn't a four-letter word, son, and it's not some blind helpless soul, like many people make love seem."

He sprayed some water onto my hair. He con-tinued: "I think what people really mean when the say 'love is blind' is that 'infatuation' is blind, or when some cat is so fixated on the idea of something, instead of the real thing, that they get mixed up."

I flipped the page of *The New York Times* article.

"It's like a lot of broads go with a cat, or a lot of cats go with some broad, cause they got some idea in their head of what the person is like."

"Sort of like a mirage you see, an oasis far off in the distance?" I asked as I read.

"Yeah, or kind of like thinking you about to be with some broad but it turns to out to be a man in hiding."

"You see the hands, you see the Adam's apple, but you ignore it all cause . . ."

"You smoked too much dope," Lev said, "or had one vodka shot too many, so you don't pay no attention to the red flags."

I stopped reading and looked at him in the mirror.

"Kind of like a $10.00 brand new Rolex on Canal street, huh?"

"Yeah," he nodded, "sort of like that, but you not sticking no pecker of yours in the fake or hot watch, but with some of them camouflaged trannies, you can get yourself into some milk chocolate sticky situation, if you catch my drift."

He looked at me and smirked.

"Sure, got your drift, cause that's not Hershey's chocolate you talking about."

"No cow's milk either," he chuckled. I did the same with him.

I went back to reading the article. It explained how some wanted to negotiate a resolution to the conflict in the outset, but that they were called "unpatriotic" or worse. Many, according to the article, considered it "political suicide" to suggest a non-violent resolution. The odd thing was, though, according to one of my pop's friends, whose son was a Navy pilot flying sorties daily, "on the one hand, they don't want to come to some negotiated resolution. One the other hand, they've got guys like my son over there fighting with one hand behind his back, not being able to hit there, not being able to attack at this time, but okay at this other time. It's a total Catch 22."

"Same stupidity, different application," cynical Lev said as he pointed his comb at the article.

"What do you mean?" I looked up at him.

"You cannot put the pecker in half way and think she not going to get pregnant. Cause right when you put it in, you can baste the turkey with your juices, da?"

"Da" means "yes" in Russian.

"Yea, I get that." I said.

"Well," he shrugged, "if you go to another country and get involved with a war, you break things. You then own the things you break. You can't put your pecker in just a little without the risk of becoming a papa."

"You mean you go all in, or stay out?" I asked.

I saw from the corner of my eyes a teen with the Asiatic black olive eyes looking over at me. I thought for sure it was Wu, the coat rack boy. I had a feeling he put the paper clip in that engagement invitation.

"No," Lev said, "cause a doctor can come do the surgery, take out a cancer from your leg, and not cut off the whole leg, da?"

"Right," I nodded.

"But before you go in like a bull in China shop and break things, you should understand what your objective is. What is mission?"

He smiled self-satisfied.

"So your point being?" I asked.

A shot of Japanese whiskey was making its rounds on a tray. The shop often got samples of the best new scotches and whiskies from custom outlets in Japan and Scotland.

"Point being is have a plan, boy," he waved his comb, "before you get yourself involved into a big soap opera called 'Vietnam,' da?"

"Da," I said.

"There were red flags before the shit hit the roller coaster in Vietnam," Lev said.

"You mean shit hit the fan?"

"Roller coaster, fan, it is the same in the end, you still have a bunch of smelly shit you need to deal with, da?"

"Da."

The Doors song "Back Door Man" was playing quietly in the background on Lev's phono record, which he allowed customers to play when they'd come, using their own records that they'd keep at the shop. Lev continued:

"Vietnam had a few red flags: the French occupation before the war, the Geneva Conference which solved nothing, and the American support of man named Ngo Diem in Hanoi who many Buddhists has the despise for. Many in South Vietnam view Americans with the same hatred as the French croissants who occupied their country for so long."

I just sat and listened.

"And when things started, there was no plan like there was when the Yankees do the invasion of France, D-Day, big plan, big boats, clearance objectives."

"Clear objectives," I corrected his English.

"Da, that, too," he said with a small smirk. "All Uncle Lev is saying is that most war is the avoidable, and that when it starts there are ways to end it, but to dangle and infatuate yourself with notion of war being glamourous, honorable, and with clear lines of engagement is to be delusional about what it is really like."

"Sort of like how some are infatuated with an asshole?" I asked.

He took the little cup of whiskey that was passed around. He shot it. He looked at me in the mirror.

"Da, like being the infatuated with the big asshole – or the big bitch." He smirked. He continued cutting. "Do you know how many men I haves in here who come to tell me about the bitch they marry,

86

and that they get away with their mistress or they 'going to shoot bitch in the head?"

"No, probably a few hundred." I flipped the page of the newspaper to another article entitled *Invisible Godfather of New York: Boxers or Briefs?*

"Eh, exactly, son, about a hundred men in here telling me of the asshole things they doing to these women, who take it and even want to seeming more, like a Pavlov dog who not never learning from Pavlov, but then then you have these men who go with the 'looker' . . ."

"Or sometimes a hooker," I interjected as I read.

"Da, da, hooker looker, and they wondering why she is doing whatever she wants, be the big Alpha Bitch, while they walk around to take the dog for walk at night, and after giving her money, she is out to do whatever she wants."

I remember the start of the *New York Times* article saying something like:

> *Boxers or briefs? What would a man who runs the country's crime syndicate, allegedly here from New York, wear? Today we asked Vogue's Editor, Diana Vreeland, her opinion.*

> *NYT: "So, Diana, do you think this Invisible Godfather of New York wears boxers or briefs?"*

Diana: Oh, darling, maybe he goes commando, you know? Too busy with all of those orders can make a man just cut to the chase, right?

I put the paper down. I wondered to myself what I'd wear if I was such a man. I probably would wear fancy tapered boxers, a mix between the tight brief and the baggy boxer. I had seen some on the market by an English maker, I think.

"Seen many of these divorces end up like civil war in Vietnam, da," Lev suddenly said. I put the newspaper on my lap.

"What you mean?" I asked.

"Eh, what can I say, many of these men thinking with the heads on their dicks, and not see the civil war in the making that they getting themselves into, where they fight for years over the kids, the houses, the stocks, all the same shit."

I nodded in agreement.

"I bet the kids just become bargaining chips," I said.

"Yeah, little cute Vegas chips that these couples use in their own versions of the Vietnam, trying to see if the next bet will get them the better deals."

"Better deal," I said.

"Da, bigger better deal, this what I mean."

"Horrible shit," I said as I read more about the suspected haunts of the Invisible Godfather.

"Da, the kids end up in therapists, take the drugs, you name it, to forgetting what it is like to be used as a Vegas bargaining chips by their own parental units. It is like a big long mental fuck."

"Mental fuck in a bad way," I said.

"Eh, son," Lev stopped and put his scissors on my shoulder, "what you think I mean to make the mental fuck in a kinky hot way?"

We chuckled.

When I heard all of this, I thought about Ella and Blake. Whose phone number was that which dropped out of his jacket at their Hamptons Party? Was that a red flag that Ella should have picked up on? Or was she so infatuated with the idea of Blake that she would ignore any red flag just to keep him on that pedestal? I wondered.

"So I always says to my clients, whenever I hear this bullshit, say: bon voyage Vietnam."

"Meaning, Lev?"

"Say goodbye to the civil war, leave it before it comes, pick up on red flags, heed them, cause when you get involved into it, is like being in the woman without no protection and you don't want to pull out cause it feels so good – but you also don't want to have baby. This is civil war of mind – conflicted. So I say bon voyage to this bullshit state of minds."

I shrugged. I then asked:

"I guess that's why they say history repeats itself."

"Da, unless you see the repetition coming and say, 'bon voyage' to it. 'In hindsight, a cliff' many of my customers is says, da, da, da."

"I guess they do say hindsight is 20/20."

"Maybe, but sometimes foreskin can be 20/20."

"Foresight."

"You have to have foreskin to have foresight that it is going to hurt like a bitch when it gets circumcised, yes?"

I giggled as I waved off his malarkey. He giggled, too.

"What if I feel like this Ella is getting herself into a civil war in the making with her fiancé? I mean, they have invited me to their engagement party, but I feel like she is going to be sorry if she marries this guy."

"Are you her papa or mama?" Lev asked as he started finishing up my cut.

"No."

"Are you her older brother?" Lev asked.

"No."

"But you are her friend?"

"Yes."

He took the Louis Vuitton inspired "Monday's" branded cape off of me. He wiped off my shoulders.

"Well, then, be her friend and listen. Got to this party of hers. Maybe you make out with one of her friends in the closet – or more? Remember," he patted me on the face, "bring some rubbers. And what she does with her life is out of your control. If she asks, you answer. Until then, is not your place."

I started to get up.

He shrugged.

"And who knows? Maybe she has guardian angel like this, what his name," he took the newspaper out of my hand and looked at the article I was just reading, "Invisible Godfather of New York that is going to looks out for her with this Bleak."

"No, Blake," I corrected him.

"That's what I said," Lev responded.

He smirked.

I threw *The New York Times* article on the fancy empty barber chair next to me. I peeked over. I saw a *Wall Street Journal* paper there. A crossword puzzle was showing. I picked it up. I peeked at the writing. It was the same neat writing I saw the last time. One of the answers across was: "dagger." But written in neat all caps handwriting was: "bugger." I looked back at Lev. He already had his next customer. It was a very fancy looking Mexican man, thick mustache, wearing a Wall Street three-piece suit, and it was none other than Money Max Sanchez, the man who I'd eventually sit down next to at the wedding. I didn't know him then, though.

Lev saw me peeking at him as he got Max ready. Lev winked at me in the mirror as Max handed him a paper bag. Lev poked his hand into the bag, picking out what looked like a latke. He pulled out some sour cream, dipped the latke into it, and savored the taste.

I gathered my things.

"Want a latke, kid?" Lev asked. "The best ones are baked just around the corner from Max's Park Avenue office."

"No thanks, Lev," maybe next time, I said. Max just sat in the chair, eyes closed, a pleased smile on his face.

I think I had just discovered for certain who this Invisible Godfather was:

Lev the sneaky cynical criminal Hyman.

The FBI raid a few days later convinced me even further.

Chapter 6

Guardian Pirate

The Saturday, October 12, 1968, headline on the front page of *New York Post* sitting atop my toilet read:

FBI Raids Office Of
Money Bags Latke
Alleged Underworld Financier!

I read the *Post* headline above as I put on my tuxedo to get ready for Ella and Blake's engagement party at The Carlyle. "Max Sanchez," I said out to Frankie, my dog, who just stared at me as he hung out on the bed. "Didn't Max bring latkes with him when he came to Lev's?" I tightened my bow tie in the mirror as Frank Sinatra's song "Moon River" played on my record player. I then picked up the newspaper off the toilet to read this:

In the wee hours on the morning of October 11, 1968, FBI agents raided the Park Avenue office of alleged underworld financier known as Money Bags Latke to get incriminating documents on his clients. To the agents' surprise, the office was empty except for boxes of freshly made latkes with fresh coffee and orange juice. According to one agent, "we were like what the f***? We get an anonymous tip this guy manages all of the money for international underworld players. But all we got was cooked latkes. I must admit, and maybe I shouldn't say this, but they were the best I've ever had. Sorry grandma."

Scratching my head, I wondered who gave them the tip? And who was this Max Sanchez character? Was Lev Hyman one of his clients? Was Sanchez this "Money Bags Latke"? That would have been ironic cause Sanchez wasn't even Jewish.

I looked at my watch. "Shit," I said. "Better get going." I kissed Frankie on the head, exited my bedroom, ran out of my apartment, and grabbed a taxi to The Carlyle on the Upper East Side. I paid my fare, got out, and headed towards the entrance of the hotel. Standing next to the entrance was Winston, Ella's butler and, as I started to figure out, her secret security. As Winston smoked a Chesterfield cigarette, a six-foot-six man stood with a black leather pirate looking patch covering his left eye. The ebony skinned man leaned down to whisper into Winston's ear. He smiled as he intently listened.

"You look like two little school girls telling secrets," I said to Winston. The pirate patched man stood back up, surveying the streets, as though I caught them colluding to invade the cookie jar.

"Good evening, Mr. Egan," Winston said as he held out his ghost white hand for me to shake.

"Good evening, Mr. Black," I said back to him as I shook his hand. Winston dripped some ash from his cigarette into the black oyster ashtray that was on the table next to him. I looked behind me. There was a line forming.

And then I heard Winston say:

"Let's see if you made the list this evening, shall we?"

I peered back in front of me. Winston put the cigarette back into his mouth. I could see the ebony skinned man smirking from the side of my eye.

Winston pulled up the guest list. He turned it around. He pointed to my name. There it was, handwritten in pencil: "Ducky." Winston pulled the list back to him. He made a mark next to my name as the ash from his cigarette flew in the wind.

"Have fun in there, Ducky," Winston looked up at me with an almost imperceptible smile.

I tipped my fedora to him.

"Mr. Ducky says thank you."

Slowly, I walked past the Chesterfield smoking butler and his ebony-skinned compatriot sporting the pirate patch. I took off my fedora and walked inside the Art Deco hotel. There was a tuxedoed security detail directing my way into Café Carlyle. I followed their open palms. When I entered into the Café, there were about thirty candle lit tables. Seated at each were tuxedoed men and their gala dressed dates. Playing the piano was Ray Charles, the blind jazz musician. Smoke from the cigarettes filled the room. It was like an aquarium filled with smoky water and drunk fish. I heard a sort of back woods Texas accented man say from my right side:

"Mr. Egan, I presume?"

I looked over. A slim-slick tuxedoed man was peering down on me. He sported a thin mustache on top of his lip and perfectly parted hair.

"Yes, yes," I nodded holding my fedora.

"Let me take that for you," he said, "I'm the maître d' of this dump, name is Taft Hardin," he held out his cowboy big hand for me to shake. I shook it. He smiled. He had some white gold fronts. I thought maybe he was raised by great whites. I handed him my fedora with my left hand.

"A pleasure," he nodded. His spring blue sky eyes stared straight at me.

"Please follow me, Mr. Egan," Taft said, waving me to come with him, a large black onyx looking ring on his left hand shining in the lights of the stage. "I'll be taking you to your place in this here circus," he looked around, his perfectly combed hair looking like it had a mix between olive oil, vermouth, and dirty salty ocean water in it. He walked as an old Mississippi man would walk on a scorching summer day, slow, deliberate, conserving his energy. We arrived at a table towards the front.

Ray Charles was playing his song "Blackjack." I looked up at him. He smiled. I don't know if it was at me. But maybe blind people can see things we don't?

Taft Hardin went over and bent down to whisper in Ella's ear as she spoke to one of her girlfriends. There was an empty chair to her left. Blake was sitting on her right. Taft looked over at me and pointed to the empty chair as he said, "your seat."

Ella paused to take a puff of her cigarette. She looked over at me as she played with her pearl necklace. Taft slowly stood back up. He did his Mississippi old man walk back over to me. "Have fun, partner," he said as his scissor length fingers with perfectly manicured fingernails patted my back slowly.

"Sure will," I patted him on his back.

He winked at me. It was like we played together when we were little.

Maybe we did play together when we were little and I just forgot.

"Oh, look what the cat dragged in," Ella said as she pushed her cigarette into the black plated Art Deco looking black oyster ash tray that was on the table.

"Cats sometimes have good taste," I said as she got up to embrace me. She kissed me on both checks, grabbing the shoulders of my tuxedo jacket almost like she was falling.

"You can say that again," she playfully patted me on the face, "come and join us." She took my hand and pulled me over to my seat.

"Blake darling, Blake darling," she said over to her fiancé, who was talking to this Max Sanchez character. Blake held up his hand for her to hold on, he nodded to Max, finished his thought, and then turned over to look at me. Max walked away.

"Greetings, there, Ducky," Blake held out his hand for me to shake.

I smiled.

"You sure do have a knack for names," I said back as I shook his hand.

"What can I say? I need a creative outlet somewhere, right?" He winked an insulting wink at me, not the same "have a swell time, partner" wink that Taft Hardin gave me.

Blake dipped some of the ash from his cigarette into the same black ashtray.

"Just in good fun, you know that, right Mickey?" Blake smiled broadly with his perfect teeth, perfect part in his hair, and perfect tuxedo tie to complement his perfect blond hair.

"Blake, Blake," a finely tuxedoed man patted Blake's shoulder, "meet my fiancé, Estelle, Harvard Business School, class of 1967. Blake turned away from me to look at the fiancé.

Ella leaned over. She whispered in my ear.

"This place is like a Harvard Business School alumni convention."

I looked around. I whispered back:

"I like *Star Trek* conventions better. At least I can dress up as Spock, you know?" I made a Vulcan salute with my left hand. Just in case you don't know what it looks like, here it is:

Ella leaned away and giggled to herself.

"Let me introduce you to my mother and brother, okay?" She said.

"No, unacceptable."

She waved me off.

"Mom, mom," she said over the table to a regal looking 53-year-old blond woman, wearing a pearl necklace like her daughter and an off the shoulder black Valentino looking gown, one I'd seen in *The New York Times* style section.

"That's me," the woman said as she held her cigarette holder, putting her hand up to Taft Hardin, who she was speaking to.

"This is Mickey, Mickey Egan, Jr., my friend I told you about," Ella said. I started to get up to walk over to Sophia Gordon, who was sitting on the other side of the table.

"Please, don't get up Mickey," she held her hand up, "we'll have time to catch up later," she took another puff of her cigarette. "Ella has told me so many lovely things about you, and I look forward to further meeting your acquaintance," she said as she held up her martini.

Just then, the flapper dressed waitress brought my martini. I took it and held it up to Sophia.

"Cheers, Mickey," Sophia said with a warm smile.

"Cheers to you, Ms. Gordon, and congratulations," I responded.

From the corner of my eye, I could see Blake peeking over with a jealous eye. I ignored him. I sipped my martini. Sophia Gordon went back to sipping her drink and to speaking with Taft.

Ella brushed my shoulder.

"And that's my brother, Otis," Ella pointed over to the black bespectacled 35-year-old or so scholarly looking man. As his long-slicked back hair dripped over his forehead, he kissed the neck of this taller Brazilian-German looking woman next to him. She was laughing and tapping him on the head with the beat of the music as she sipped her drink.

"And that's his wife, Catarina," Ella whispered in my ear as she nodded towards the Brazilian-German stunner. "She used to be a fashion model but now she is the head of marketing at a major Madison Avenue firm."

I looked at Ella.

"Which firm?"

Ella shrugged and sipped her drink.

"The one that Otis is a partner at." Ella looked at me. We laughed together. "You'll get to know Otis later, I am sure," she then nodded. I adjusted myself in my seat after twisting to peek over at Otis and Catarina. The rest of the seats at the table were empty. I presumed those attendees were dancing.

"So what have you been doing with yourself lately? I haven't seen you in a while?" Ella pulled out another cigarette. I pulled out my Zippo lighter. I lit her up.

"I've been doing plenty with myself," I said as I got her cigarette lit, "but I don't know if you really want to know the details."

She leaned back. She took a long drag.

"Silly goose, you know what I mean."

Ray Charles was now playing "Night Time Is The Right Time."

"Yeah," I played with the water in front of me. "Been hanging at my barber shop, one of the most interesting places in the city. Ever heard of a place called *Monday's*?"

"Sure," she nodded and adjusted her pearl necklace, "Mondays come after Sundays."

"Yeah, yeah, well," I leaned over to whisper into her ear, "I think the owner of the joint is this invisible Godfather of New York that I've been reading about in the newspaper." I leaned back to confirm nobody was listening.

She looked over at me with her pale blues.

"You think so?" She put her left hand on my right forearm.

I shrugged.

"I can't tell, but you remember that mustached Sergeant Amos from the train? The one who came to investigate the theft of your pen?"

"Yeah," she said.

"Well, I saw him there, he's the customer of *Monday's.*"

"Who owns that place?" Ella asked.

I leaned over.

"A guy named Lev Hyman," I said quietly.

"Lev, Lev Hyman," she sat and said to herself, "that name sounds so familiar." She stared at Mr. Charles, who was playing "Tell The Truth" on the piano. This time he was backed by a bassist and a horn player.

Ella snapped her fingers. She looked over at me.

"I know where I've heard that name, my mom's financial advisor, he goes to get his haircuts from Lev Hyman."

She dipped some of her cigarette into the black oyster ashtray.

"Oh yeah, and who is your mom's financial advisor?"

Ella leaned over even closer to me.

"His name is Maximillian Sanchez, but we call him Money Max," she said with a smirk.

"Did I hear the magic words?" Blake interrupted by putting his hand on Ella's and sticking his head over her plates. He stared at both of us.

She looked over at him and broke a half-hearted smile. I did the same.

"That guy Max, he's magic, I'm so glad your mom introduced me to him," Blake said as he took Ella's drink and took a long sip. "He has an eye for spotting quality in the most undervalued filth in the marketplace."

"Maybe that's why they call him Money Max," Ella smiled at me.

"Yeah, well, he sure is money, I tell you, I mean, I don't think we would have found our apartment without his real estate connections," Blake said as he took another long sip of Ella's drink.

She tapped him on his arm.

"You sure have changed your tune since you first met him," Ella said as she took her drink back.

"Pray tell," I said to her as I sipped mine. She looked over at me.

"Max went to Harvard Business School with Blake, but they didn't even know each other there and, the thing is, my family's been doing business with his since way back," she puffed her cigarette.

"Come on," Blake said as he grabbed Ella's drink back, "I always thought he was a great dresser, never doubted that much." He took a long swig.

I stared at Blake as he drank. His family was old money. Ella's mother's family was, too, or so I've gathered reading some *New York Times* articles written by my cousin Hank. But from the same articles, I also learned that Ella's father, Jacky, was a Marseille born French Mafia type who was a "black money billionaire." He fought with the Allies during World War II. I think Ella was a French Resistance love baby, a romantic tryst between Sophia Gordon and this Jacky, who is reported to have died during the war. And so Ella's family's money was a little bit old and a little bit new. Whereas Blake's was just old. So I could see why Blake would shy away from using a financial advisor like Money Max, even though he went to Harvard Business School. I'm sure Blake would use reasons like: "he's not Jewish," "he is Jewish," "he's Mexican," "he's not from the South," or "he looks part Jewish."

"Regardless of what I thought about him during school or when I first met him," Blake put Ella's drink on the table, "I thought differently when I started to see the returns on the investments he made for my family." Blake started kissing Ella's hand.

The thing is, Ella told me during one of our coffees at Café Reggio in Greenwich Village that she thought Blake didn't like her mother. "I think Blake's threatened by her," she told me, "a wild card in his book." Plus, she once said sadly, "I know Blake doesn't like my brother Otis." I remember asking: "why?" She said something like, "cause he doesn't fit into Blake's box. So he's not vulnerable to Blake's manipulative mind games."

"Speaking of investment advisors," I said to Ella as Blake kissed her hand, "did you hear about this recent story of the FBI raiding some 'Money Bags Latke' only to find freshly baked latkes?" I smirked in amusement at the story.

Blake stopped kissing Ella's hand.

"Yeah, well," Blake snapped his fingers trying to get the attention of the waitress, "I don't think it is so funny to make fun of the FBI. Cause whoever made that tip to the FBI was risking his life to get some justice around here," Blake looked at the waitress as he pointed to the martini glass with his index finger. The waitress took his cue.

I sat wondering: how did Blake know the tipster was a man? I also wondered if Blake's resentment for Ella's family would have caused him to bite the hand that feeds him by making such a call to the FBI. But, even if he did, who tipped off Money Bags Latke that the FBI was coming?

Suddenly, a long slender tuxedoed arm made its way in front of me. The left hand with the black onyx ring on it grabbed the black oyster ashtray and started to clean it. I looked up. It was Taft Hardin.

"Enjoying yourself, there, partner?" He asked.

I nodded to the rest of the table.

"Yeah," I asked him to come a little closer with my index finger. He did. "But there is a little too much riff-raff in here, don't you say?"

"That's what I say," he shrugged as he put the clean black oyster ashtray on the table. "Then again, sometimes it takes time for the cream to rise to the top of the cowboy coffee, don't you say?" He patted me on the back. He leaned back. I could see Blake and Ella talking in an excited way from the corner of my eye.

"How'd you get tied up with this gang?" I asked Taft. He straightened his tie. He shrugged.

"My family was from Illinois, way back, came to San Francisco, and ended up doing business with Ella's family before there was phones."

I asked Taft to come closer again. He bent down.

"You mean with her father's family?"

He smirked at me.

"That's what I hear," he patted me on the back.

My pop, Mickey Egan Sr., was based in Paris during the war and did intelligence work for the Allies, along with doing security for some night club there. So I asked Taft:

"Who knows? Maybe your family and mine have done business too, don't you say?"

"Possibly," he said as he winked at me. "Excuse me. Got to tend to some things in that there kitchen." As he slowly walked away, I could hear Ella and Blake arguing in the background. I just kept staring at the stage where Ray Charles and his quintet were playing "Heartbreaker." I acted like I was just listening to the music and not Ella and Blake. I bobbed my head. And then I heard Ella say with a mix of anger and sadness:

"I thought it was junk mail in the start, junk mail from some pirate soliciting investments into his Ponzi scheme. But then I realized: it was a statement for one your secret bank accounts! I thought we agreed to be transparent?"

I closed my eyes, sipped my drink, and bobbed my head even more to the song.

"Come on," I heard Blake say as the waitress put another martini on the table, "that money is for our kids, for their college, I swear." He started to sip his martini.

I did some air drumming on the table with my index fingers.

"Blake, don't play me for the fool. There was more than $4,000,000.00 in the account!"

"Who the hell mailed that to you anyway, it was none of your business," his strategy seemingly changing from this is our kids' college fund to its none of your business. "There are only a few people I can think of who had access to that account."

I remember acting like I was playing the trumpet.

"I don't remember who sent it, but I think the address was on Park Avenue," I could hear her light up another cigarette.

"Park Avenue you don't say?" Blake said in an angry way thinking.

Suddenly, a fast song, "Tell Me How Do You Feel," came on. I opened my eyes. More people started dancing. Max Sanchez came up to the table.

"Come on! You guys are so boring gringo! Ella: let's dance!" He held out his hand. She looked at Blake and put out her cigarette.

"Let's," she said.

I opened my eyes. Blake looked angrily at Ella and Max as they went to the dance floor. I looked over across the table. And who was there staring in my direction with a Cheshire cat grin as his wife licked his neck? It was none other than:

Otis Gordon:

Was he Ella's guardian pirate?

Chapter 7

Pants Around His Ankles

Invisible Godfather of New York
Implicated in Bank Robbery
Of More Than $4,000,000.00!

The headline above from *The New York Times* stared at me when I woke up the following Monday morning, October 14, 1968, to take Frankie for a walk. The *Times* was on top of the stack of newspapers delivered to my apartment every morning. I picked *The New York Post* out of the stack. This was their headline:

Invisible Crossword Puzzle Godfather
Mugs Prominent Financier Out
Of His Lunch Money!

Scratching my head, I stared at the stack of newspapers. I whispered to myself: "$4,000,000.00? That was Blake Stimson's dough?" Frankie's bark took me out of my reverie. I grabbed the stack of newspapers and went back with Frankie into the apartment. Sitting at the small kitchen table with my coffee, I opened up *The Wall Street Journal* to read about the $4,000,000.00 heist:

> *When Blake Stimson, a New Orleans born financier, went to check his bank account at City National Bank this past Saturday morning, he was shocked. "I couldn't believe it! Shards of old newspaper crossword puzzles were splattered all over the vault floor. The answers weren't even right. So stupid! The bank manager didn't know how they got there. So we called the FBI," says Mr. Stimson, who is engaged to Ms. Ella Gordon, a local socialite.*

> *Next, we spoke to Dr. Nicky Robinson, head of FBI's financial crimes unit based in Brooklyn. He had visited the bank just a week before investigating another theft. According to Dr. Robinson: "Yeah, man, totally weird. We went into the vault, and it was like, whoa! The cash was all counterfeit! Supposing nobody had ever checked it? Anyway, someone at some*

112

point lifted the real cash and replaced it with those counterfeits—or maybe it was counterfeit all along? On the down low, I'll tell you, those counterfeits were the best I've ever seen, stunning like, what's her name, that super model Naomi Sims, you know? We suspect it was the invisible Godfather of NYC, cause he gets off on crappy crossword puzzle answers. Total oddball. Probably fills out puzzles with his pants around his ankles in the dirty John."

When this paper asked the bank manager, Mrs. Belle Francis, how the shards of crossword puzzles got onto the vault floor, she answered: "well, I can tell you, whoever filled those puzzles out is a total idiot, cause the answers were wrong, so wrong. I mean, we found crossword puzzle chards in the ventilation shaft that led to the vault which were just so absurd. I am an avid crossword puzzle fan, and, frankly, whoever did this angered me greatly with his disrespect of the crossword craft. Who does he think he is?"

Suddenly, the phone rang. It was Ella.

"Shit, shit, its all over the papers!" She said in a sort of whisper.

"You mean the pigeon hit your paper, too?" I smirked as I sipped my coffee.

"Come on, Mickey, I'm serious, this is serious," she said like she was looking around. I gathered she was still in her apartment with Blake.

"Yeah, yeah," I kept browsing through *The Wall Street Journal* article, "but what the hell do you want me to do? I just found out about it myself." I smirked. I didn't let her know that I overheard her and Blake talking about that $4,000,000.00 bank statement. I had left without saying goodbye. I was tired of their drama.

I could hear Ella nervously puff her cigarette.

"Only three people knew about that account," she said thinking, "Max, Blake, and then me. So it had to be Max. What do you think?"

I shrugged. I stared at the name "Naomi Sims" in the *Journal* article. I knew she was a top black model slated to be the cover of *Life Magazine*. Word had it was that she was dating the son of the owner of the 21 Club in New York City. I then said:

"It was this Nicky Robinson character from the FBI that did it," I smirked.

"What? Come on. Be serious," she said. I could hear her ash her cigarette.

"I am being serious," I said.

She paused over the phone.

114

"Well, can I tell you something?" This time she whispered into the phone.

"I already know your sign, Ella," I said.

"I'm sort of happy this happened," she confided.

"You mean this shit all over the papers?" I asked.

She paused again to smoke. She ignored me.

"You seem to have a lot of red flags on your road that you have been ignoring?" It was more of a statement than a question.

She ignored me again.

"Our wedding rehearsal party is at the 21 Club," she said.

"The XXX bar?"

"You can get to know Otis and his wife better," she responded, ignoring me XXX comment.

"If they get to know each other any better, they'd be glued," I said.

She ignored me.

"You'll get the invite in the next few days."

"And what about the red flags?" I said.

"Normal growing pains. They happen in every relationship."

I just sat and listened.

"But you wouldn't know about that, would you?" She said.

"I prefer the red flags on the beach to the red flags you are ignoring. Plus," I looked over to Frankie and made a kissy sound, "growing pains are like teething for a kid who gets stronger molars after, not weaker ones full of cavities."

She was silent.

"I'll see you at the rehearsal, smart ass."

She hung up.

I know I had hit a chord. But maybe she needed that chord to be hit.

A few days later, I received the wedding rehearsal invitation. It read:

> The Future Mr. and Mrs. Stimson
> Wedding Rehearsal Dinner
> At the 21 Club
> New York City
> Friday, July 11, 1969
> 7:00 p.m. – 9:00 p.m.
> RSVP Required

I thought to myself: are they going to practice going down the aisle at the 21 Club? Or are they going to even practice at all? I supposed it didn't matter. From the time of our talk that morning about the red flags and the wedding rehearsal dinner, Ella and I had many coffees, teas, and martinis, but never did she mention the therapist girl or the $4,000,000.00

bank account. It was like these things never happened. Little did I know at the time that this Invisible Godfather of New York, whoever it was, wasn't only implicated in the theft of her pen, but also in planting these flags that she ignored.

During the wedding rehearsal party that humid July night in the summer of 1969, I got closer to unmasking this invisible New York pirate once and for all.

Chapter 8

Toilet Humor

"Between me, you, and my cigarette, unfortunately I don't particularly care for them," Sophia leaned over and said quietly to me through the thick cigarette smoke as we sat at the 21 Club. I remember her saying this as she peered over to Blake's family's table. Sophia used the cigarette smoke as her camouflage.

I looked at her. She didn't look at me. I admired her reserved candor. Someone else may have called them: "assholes." But Sophia was poignantly reserved.

I had arrived at the 21 Club on 52nd Street in New York City around 7:00 p.m. that July 11th night in 1969. If you don't know anything about the restaurant, which I am pretty sure you don't, the restaurant is a Prohibition style speakeasy founded on January 1, 1930. Since then, it has passed through several owners. It was a frequented by Frank Sinatra, among others.

As with Ella's other events, ivory skinned Winston was out front with the ebony skinned pirate-patched man. From the look of the guest list, I think Sophia had taken over.

"It seems that they finally took spelling lessons," Winston didn't even spend time greeting me as he turned the guest list around to show me, his manicured finger pointing to my name.

He whispered something to his taller voodoo looking compatriot as he did.

"It looks like they did," I peeked at the guest list, pleased that my name was finally spelled correctly. This time it was typewritten.

The pirate eye patched man chucked. Winston did, too.

I peeked at Winston. He winked across the street. I looked behind me. Nothing was there. Nobody was there. But then I remember looking above. In the twilight of the afternoon, I saw the shine of what I thought was perhaps a sniper scope.

"Looking ravishing tonight, Mr. Egan," Winston said as he admired my tuxedo. "Is your suit from England?" The pirate eye patched man copped a feel, too, of the lapel. I turned back around to look at the ebony-ivory duo.

"Yeah, but don't tell anybody: my tux is a hand me down from my old man."

Winston leaned over.

"Looks smashing on you." He patted me on the shoulder. "Now get in there and drink some martinis for us," he leaned back out and handed his associate a cigarette, after which Winston took one for himself. As I walked inside the 21 Club, I remember back to one time when my old man took me to the Napoleon House, a bar in New Orleans not far from Pirate's Alley. The bar had a haunted feel to it. Winston reminded me of that bar. Maybe it was because Edward Thatch, the Caribbean pirate known as Black Beard, was English, like Winston.

When I walked inside the 21 Club, Dean Martin and Sammy Davis, Jr., had a quintet behind them. They were singing "Volare." Cigarette smoke bellowed throughout the air. A young handsome milk chocolate skinned man greeted me.

"And you must be Mr. Egan?"

"Yea, yea, last time I checked," I answered.

"Come with me and I'll show you to your seat." The finely coiffed goateed man touched my forearm in a friendly way. I walked slowly with him. He was wearing a sharp Italian suit, one that I'd seen many of my pop's friends wear when they came over for dinner.

As I walked, it looked like there were the who's who of New York's VIP sitting in the midst of the swampy looking cigarette smoke. Mayor Lindsay and even governor Nelson Rockefeller were there.

We arrived at a circular table that was just next to where Mr. Martin and Mr. Davis Jr. were singing. It was quite intimate. Sitting at the table was Sophia, Ella, Otis, and his wife Catarina.

"Well, well, a sight for sore eyes," Ella put her cigarette holder down. She got up. She kissed me softly on both cheeks. I surveyed the table. It was full of empty martini glasses and old fashions.

"I wouldn't have missed this for the world," I said to Ella.

"Except if you got front row Yankee tickets," she said patting my back.

"Well, yea, not that," I smirked as we hugged.

"I see you are in good hands," the milk chocolate skinned man said as he patted my back.

"I don't know," I said, "I'll tell you at the end of the night."

"Thanks Nicky," Ella said to the man. I didn't think anything of the name "Nicky" until later on. "Come on and sit down," she said pointing to my open seat, which was in between her and her mother, who was seated to my right. Otis and his wife Catarina were sitting across the table.

A waiter came by. I ordered a gin martini.

"Mom, mom," Ella said over my plate setting to her mother, who was busy speaking to the governor. "Mom, mom," Ella said again. Sophia finished up her chat with the governor, patting his forearm, and turned to look at me.

"Are you the pool boy or am I imagining someone else?" Sophia smirked as she smoked the cigarette from her cigarette holder.

"I'm not the pool boy, Ms. Gordon, I'm the brick layer," I said as I pulled up my chair to the table.

She looked below the table. When she got back up, she asked:

"Then where are you boots, son?" She leaned over and playfully tapped my shoulder. She then kissed me on both cheeks, as if we were in Paris. "Glad you could make it, Mickey," she said as she pulled me closer with her hands on my back, "a little fresh air."

"I try," I said.

We broke our embrace. The waiter delivered the gin martini. "Thank you," I said.

Suddenly, I heard from the across the table in a slurred tone from Otis:

"At least one of us around here has some brains."

I wasn't sure if he meant himself or me, but I guess that was how he was, intentionally ambiguous unless he didn't want to be. With a rascal smirk plastered on his face, Otis raised his martini glass, tuxedo tie untied, his wife doing the same with her martini glass.

I raised my glass back to Otis and Catarina. Without any pause after sipping their drinks, they went back to their little world with one another, her rubbing his hair and messing up the otherwise fancy part, him mussing up her hair so that it was a knitting project gone awry.

"That was quick," I said over to Ella and then looked at Sophia.

"You haven't seen anything yet with him," Ella said in sort of exasperation but also with a tinge of appreciation. "Check out his socks."

I looked underneath the table. Otis was wearing fancy slip on black loafers. His socks were bright hot pink. I looked back up at Ella and Sophia. I smirked.

Suddenly, the mayor of New York city came by to speak to Ella. As he leaned over to speak to her, she grabbed my forearm. I looked off into the distance across from where Mr. Martin and Mr. Davis Jr. were playing. I spotted Blake Stimson's family's table. There was the matriarch and patriarch, sitting with their backs straight, along with Blake's brothers and their wives. When I saw them all sitting, not smoking or drinking, I thought of Ken and Barbie, the plastic toy dolls.

Ella pulled my forearm.

"Mayor Lindsay," she said, "this is one of my dearest friends, Mickey Egan, Jr., a professor of philosophy at Brooklyn College."

My pop was a nightclub entrepreneur during World War II in Paris, among other places, and my mom worked at a non-profit. Needless to say, I didn't feel among the crème of the crop at the party.

"A pleasure, Mickey, a pleasure," the mayor leaned over to shake my hand.

"Nice to meet you, Mayor Lindsay," I said.

We broke our handshake. Ella went back to speaking with the mayor, her hand resting comfortably on my forearm. Suddenly, I heard Sophia ask me:

"How did you like the Ray Charles show at The Carlyle?"

I turned to look at her. Even though I didn't feel like the crème of the crop at the party, Sophia made me feel otherwise.

"I loved it. I was wondering who was able to get him to play?"

"The owner of this place."

"Who's that?"

"An old friend, named Don Robinson."

"Don Robinson?"

"Oh, yes, he's an entrepreneur, a partner in various businesses ranging from air conditioning and heating to a luxurious club called "Tijuana" in Brighton Beach."

When I heard air conditioning and heating, I thought back to the article I had read about Blake Stimson's vault break in and how the crossword puzzle chards came through the air conditioner vent. I suspect it was this FBI agent, Nicky, who fed the chards into the vent. Breaking from my internal dialogue, I finally said:

"Mr. Robinson must be connected."

She nodded her head.

I didn't think anything of the name at the time. I was too fixated on my memory of the show that Mr. Charles had put on at The Carlyle.

"Amazing how a blind man can play like that," I said.

"Yeah, well," she sipped her martini in a sort of a somber tone, "sometimes those without eyes can see things more clearly than the ones who have them."

I played with the olives in my martini.

"Einstein the playboy lion tamer once said something like, 'we worship the rational mind. But the intuitive mind is in fact the captain. The rational mind should be the trusted servant. We have it backwards.'"

Sophia giggled.

"Well, someone needs to send my daughter's rational mind to finishing school. I don't think Choate and Yale did enough for it."

"Maybe she can go back to take some more classes?"

Sophia giggled to herself even more. As Ella's hand came off of my left forearm, Sophia's hand rested softy on my right.

"She reminds me of myself when I was younger," Sophia puffed her cigarette.

"Stunning and smart?" I said and sipped my just almost too strong martini.

"You are a doll," Sophia said to me. "But, no, I don't know if Ella told you this, but I was married once before I met Ella's father, to a man actually from Blake's family."

The band was now playing "Mambo Italiano." As Mr. Martin sang the lyrics, "a girl went back to Napoli, because she missed the scenery, the native dances and the charming songs, but wait a minute, something's wrong," Sophia tapped her hand on my right forearm.

"My first husband was perfect on paper, all of the credentials, Oxford, the right family, the right bank account, the right friends," Sophia confided.

"But?" I looked over at her.

"I thought that all made the man, but I realized later that what's on paper isn't necessarily what's in the man. It was a lesson I had to learn the hard way."

A waiter came by. I pointed to Sophia's martini. She nodded. I held my fingers up for two more. The waiter nodded.

"And Ella's father?" I asked.

"Oh, yes," she put another cigarette into her cigarette holder, "he was a doll, but if you saw him you'd have thought he was Lucifer in the flesh."

"Why? Cause he liked the Mets?"

We giggled.

"No, silly goose, he was the Paris based Don of a Mafia family from Marseille, ran their nightclubs, rough business, at night. But his front during the day was being a filthy looking chain-smoking janitor at my son's elementary school."

"Otis's school?"

She nodded.

"Dirty fingernails, unshaven, cowboy coffee, cynical eyes, and so rude, just never said anything to anybody," Sophia said.

"But?"

She looked over at me.

"My son loved him. And kids are like dogs. They haven't been brainwashed yet with the way they should think, so they tell you the truth. Plus, I found out he was the chief spy for MI6's Paris station."

"Lucifer?"

"Yeah, him," Sophia giggled.

The waiter came and put our martinis on the table. We did a cheers. I looked over at Blake's family's table. They all looked sort of angry as they peered over at Otis, who was obliviously sharing a cigarette with his wife out of her cigarette holder. He was bobbing his head to the music, she was sort of pushing his head up and down to the beat, and they were both smirking.

I looked over at Sophia. She stood expressionless and stared at Blake's family. Her hand had stopped bobbing on my forearm.

"What happened to Lucifer?" I asked to get her out of her brewing anger.

She leaned her head towards me in the way you would to someone when watching a love scene in a movie.

"He disappeared," she said as she took a sip of the martini with her right hand, left hand starting to tap my forearm to the music again. "I think the Nazis got him. Last time I saw him was in Deauville, France."

Her hand tapped even more happily on my forearm now.

"And his name?"

She looked over at me while she tapped.

"Jacky," she sipped, "Jacky Bonaparte."

Suddenly, my small head told me I needed a toilet trip.

"Excuse me please," I said, "I have to use the restroom.

She nodded.

"No," she grinned.

I got up and traveled through the cigarette smoke, cigar smoke, high-end perfumes, laughs, darlings, martini smell, old fashioned smell, bar tenders cleaning glasses, to the toilet. When I arrived into the men's toilet, which was adorned with murals, I could see cigarettes, cigars, cologne, breath mints, chewing gum, and what looked a few boxes of high end women's perfume stacked neatly underneath the sink, including Chanel No. 5.

I went to sit down on the toilet. I closed the door. A minute or so after sitting, I heard someone sit next to me. I could not see who it was. But I heard the man horribly mumble a song. He had no rhythm. It sounded like he was drunk. I think the song was "Stormy Weather." So I am sitting there, and this guy is doing the worst rendition of the song I've ever heard, and it sounded like he was busy. Then, suddenly, he flushes the toilet, drops a newspaper on the floor, pulls up his pants, and leaves. Didn't think anything of it.

That's until I looked down at *The Wall Street Journal* he dropped.

It was the *Journal's* crossword puzzle.

The answers were all filled out.

They were all wrong. Horribly wrong. All had something to do with sex.

"Boner" instead of "loner," "ecstasy" instead of "primacy."

I recognized the handwriting. It was the same handwriting as the one I saw at Lev's. All caps. I picked up the paper. As I did, I heard the sink water. This man, who was for sure the invisible Godfather of New York City, was just sitting right next to me. I dropped the paper, flushed the toilet, tended to myself, pulled up my pants as fast as I could, and then rushed out of the stall.

"May I help you?" Asked a finely dressed man as he turned on the sink for me to use.

I looked around. Nobody was in the bathroom other than me and this very tall tuxedoed man whose milk chocolate colored skin resembled that of Nicky, the man who walked me to Ella Gordon's table.

"Yeah, um, sure," I said with the newspaper in my hand, "did you just see a man leave the stall next door?"

"I did not, sorry son," he picked up a bar of what looked like fancy English soap. He held it out for me to use.

I put the newspaper in my tuxedo jacket. I took the soap and washed my hands. The tuxedoed man started arranging the cigarettes, cigars, and other items. He collected the wad of cash that was sitting next to them from the silver played Tiffany looking case.

As I washed my hands, the man asked:

"Liking the music, young man?"

"Oh, yeah, loving it," I said sort of shaking my head. "But I just wanted to ask again, cause I think it was a friend of mine, you didn't see someone leave the toilet next to me?"

"No, son," he said as he counted the cash, placing it in his jacket, "I just got here."

He then looked at me and grinned.

I finished washing my hands. I put the soap back into its holder. The man held out a towel for me to use.

"Thank you," I said, "mister?"

"Oh, yes," he said as he moved some lint off the sink, making sure it was perfect. "Name is Don, but friends call me DR."

"Why, cause you are an MD?" I said as I finished drying my hands, putting the used towel into the hamper.

"Nah, son, cause my last name is Robinson." He held out his long right hand with piano player long fingers. "And you are?"

I paused. So this was the owner of the 21 Club? Was this Robinson related to FBI agent Dr. Nicky Robinson I read about in the newspaper? And was the 21 Club chocolate skinned "Nicky" who Ella knew so well the same Dr. Nicky Robinson who was head of FBI's financial crimes division based in Brooklyn?

As I pondered these questions, I heard Ella and Blake fighting outside the bathroom door. She said something like "you know I don't wear Chanel No.

5, you bastard. Whose perfume bottle was that left in our bedroom?"

"Oh, come on, you know I get the maid perfume for Christmas. She probably left it in there after freshening up. Stop being such a paranoid conspiracy theorist," he said condescendingly.

"Oh, yeah, um," I finally said back to the towering Don Robinson back in the men's toilet, "name is Mickey, Mickey Egan Jr.," I said as I shook his hand.

"Well, enjoy the rest of your night, Mr. Egan," he said.

We broke our handshake.

As I walked outside the men's restroom, Winston Black was walking in.

"Enjoy the toilet humor, old boy?" He asked.

"Oh, yeah, couldn't get enough," I said.

Blake and Ella had disappeared.

When I went back out into the main room of the 21 Club, Mr. Davis Jr. and Mr. Martin were singing the song "Route 66." I went to sit back at the Gordon's table. But they were all on the dancefloor. As she danced with her mother, Ella had a sort of sad desperately trying to turn happy face. It looked like she had just been punched in the stomach. Otis had his head resting on Catarina's shoulder, cigarette dangling from her cigarette holder from his mouth. I sat down at the table to finish my drink. The waiter came by to change the paper on the table for the next course.

As I sat there drinking, I spotted a part of the paper that the waiter was taking away. There was writing on it in blue pen. The waiter started taking the paper off the table to throw it away.

"Wait a minute, would you mister?" I held my hand up.

"Sure, kid," the waiter said, "what you want to draw some more pictures?"

"Huh?" I said as I moved closer to him.

The waiter held up the part of the paper that was on the table. But I couldn't tell if the paper with the blue ink chicken scratch on it was in front of Otis, Sophia, or Catarina. I also didn't know if someone maybe came and drew on the paper while the Gordons were dancing, someone like Winston the butler.

On the paper was a very unflattering drawing of Blake Stimson's father, to say the very least. Below it, in the same handwriting that was on the crossword puzzle, was written this:

Dweeb, Inc. CEO.

Obviously, the artist was the invisible Godfather of New York City. He had to be the one responsible for that pen theft on the train, the paper clip trick, and the rest of the shenanigans I've relayed to you throughout the story.

At Ella's wedding that following Sunday, July 13, 1969, the day I started my story on, I'd finally unmask Ella's guardian pirate.

Or, more accurately, he'd unmask himself.

Chapter 9

Just A Little Tongue

"**Y**ou bastard! You son of an absolute certified asshole! I'm going to kill you."

That's what Ella's eyes said to me the day of the wedding. They beamed down on me from the altar on that 13th day of July in 1969. I knew what Ella's eyes said not because I stared back at her. As I mentioned earlier, I nonchalantly looked away at the pigeons on the stoop when she gazed at me. One thing I didn't mention is that the pigeons took off. They left a mountain of poop there. The poop said to me exactly what Ella was thinking.

So like a kid who has to take his medicine, I turned my head to look back at fuming Ella. Her eyes were still there, snow on the street you wish was gone after spring has officially begun.

But then something happened. And I'll never forget it.

Smash!

A smash of a wine or champagne glass on the church floor made the wedding which was otherwise full of class seem a little country crass. But in the midst of all the craziness, women looking on the floor, cops with their coffees talking about the recent Yankee game with cigarettes in their mouths, FBI agents taking witness statements while checking out some of the younger women in attendance, and Ella staring down at me, nobody seemed to notice that glass smash. Certainly, Blake didn't. He was nervously rubbing his forehead speaking with the Chief of the New York City police department.

But Ella and I noticed.

Some people know classical music and can hear chords you'll never notice. And for some reason, Ella and I were on a wavelength where the sound of the smashed glass was an accent chord. But it was a chord that others were too busy to hear.

Suddenly, she stopped peering down at me in anger. She looked over towards where the glass broke. I looked over, too. The sound came from the front of the row where Sophia, Otis, and Catarina were sitting.

"Have some more, we're going to be here for a while, hombre," Max said pushing the flask to my chest.

"Yeah, I need some," I took a humongous swig of the tequila. I handed him back the flask. He seemed to secretly enjoy the show.

"Did someone take their top off? I can get some beads," Max joked dryly as he swigged his tequila, "what's going on over there?"

I nodded my head over to Sophia, Otis, and Catarina. I felt like a National Geographic tour director showing my guest through the exotic animals in sub-Saharan Africa. Maybe that's because Ella's family was a bunch of exotic animals.

"Whoa, it's like a peyote trance," Money Max said as he looked over at Otis. "Ooh, shit," he said as he pushed the flask back to my chest, two boys watching our first peep show, "what's that on his tongue?" Max slapped my shoulder a few times with the back of his hand, "ooh, damn, give me back that flask." He grabbed it from my hand before I could take a swig. My mouth was agape in shock.

With everyone around them preoccupied talking, gossiping, or crying at the notion that the multimillion dollar platinum rings were stolen, Otis's weasel tongue peaked out of its shell. A tortoise's head couldn't move any slower. As Sophia calmly stared at her daughter standing on the altar, I winced to look more closely at Otis's tongue. It was the length of a baby lizard and but the width of a red wood.

"Shit," Money Max said to me, "guess Catarina never really needed to guess what his pecker looked like with a tongue like that, eh?" He passed the flask back to me. I smirked. "What's that shit on his tongue, a piercing? So avant-garde, right?" He asked with a slightly jealous tone.

"No," I looked even more closely, finishing the flask of tequila as Max held out a second one for me to sip on, taking the empty one from my hand, a long-distance runner in the Boston Marathon who doesn't care if he's last as long as he is smiling shit-faced. "I think it's the rings!"

I looked back at Money Max.

He took the flask full of tequila back.

"I need that," he said and sipped, nervous. He then said, "you think it is," with his hand on my forearm, a granny hanging out of her apartment window wondering what's going between a couple on the Brooklyn street below.

"Yeah," I said to Max and then stared back at Otis. He kept his tongue out long enough for Ella to see the rings, and then pushed his tortoise head of a tongue back into his mouth. Catarina was standing next to him, playing with her loose ends, seeming like she was expecting this all along and waiting for the organized shenanigan to be over.

Then Otis smirked. It was not big enough to take a photo of, but not so small that you'd miss it if you were on the wavelength that we were on.

I looked back up at Ella. She stared intently at her brother. For a moment, I could see her fists clinch. I thought she was going to rush down from the altar and murder Otis.

"Shit, she going to murder him! We better get ready," Money Max said. He handed me his one of his newspapers, as if we could use that as a weapon. I looked down at the newspaper, and I couldn't believe it. A crossword puzzle was on it. Hand written in caps on it in the exact same writing I had seen at the 21 Club was:

BETTER

THAN

THE

CIRCUS

I looked over at Max. He held his newspaper at the ready as if it was a baton. I don't think he was aware of the writing on the newspaper crossword puzzle he gave me. I looked back up at Ella. In about a minute, while her fists were still clinched, in a "I'm going to murder you" way, tears started brewing in her eyes. The tears started slow, dripping real quiet, and then they started dripping even stronger. When she looked back towards me, her fists had loosened, and a waterfall of tears were dripping down her face.

It was the first time I had seen her take her guard down and cry.

She then put her hands on her face. Her eyes closed.

"Damn, man," Money Max whispered, "we can get her some replacement rings, I mean, right? But, then again, maybe they went missing for a reason," he looked over at me mysteriously and nudged me.

I looked back over at him.

Was this a set-up?

A con?

One big shenanigan?

I didn't know. I did know that Ella was standing there, naked in the wind, and I felt for her. I thought all of the red flags, the pen, the therapist girl number, the hidden bank account, and the perfume all caught up with her infatuation.

"I don't think it's just the rings, Max," I peered at him as I handed him the newspaper.

"You think?" He asked sarcastically.

I looked back up at Ella. I walked up to the altar. I took her hands off of her face.

"Let's go outside through the back door and get some fresh air," I said looking into her wet, smeared, and sad eyes.

She nodded without saying a word. She took my hand. We walked slowly through the back door. As we did, I looked back to make sure nobody saw us. But sitting there in the front row was Sophia, Otis, and Catarina. They were all speaking to one another in a huddle, looking over our way.

When Ella and I got outside, the bright summer sun shined on our faces. The honking of the taxis on New York City's streets welcomed us as parrots would in a jungle. Honking was a relief.

Ella put her head on my shoulder. She cried like I've never heard anybody cry before.

"I just realized I've made the biggest mistake of my life," she said as her arms went around my back, pulling me close.

"Is that because you didn't bring your sunglasses?" I said dryly as I took out my handkerchief and gave it to her. I pulled out my Ray-Ban Club Master sunglasses and handed them to her.

She took the hanker chief and blew her nose. She put the sunglasses on. She then looked at me. A little sun peeking through the clouds, she looked at me with a small smile:

"I think I just figured out who stole the pen that Blake gave to me," she said blowing her nose again.

"Oh, yeah, it was a New York City police officer," I said.

"But I know who was behind him."

"Another cop," I smirked.

Out of the corner of my eye, I spotted a black Rolls-Royce. Standing in front of it reading a newspaper with a cigarette in his mouth was Winston, Ella's butler.

"I need to get out of here," she said, "to take a ride by the river, I feel like I am going to faint," she said taking some lint off of my shoulder.

"Sure, yeah, I see Mr. Black over there," I leaned over her shoulder. She looked back at him. I took her hand and we started walking towards him.

"Mr. Black, Mr. Black," I said as we walked.

"Need some more candles for the ceremony, Mr. Egan?" Winston said dryly as he put the newspaper down and looked up at me and Ella.

"Yeah, yeah, you mind taking us on a candle run to the local bodega?"

He looked at his watch.

"I think I have some time for that," he said as he put his cigarette out and threw his newspaper on top of the passenger seat of the car.

"Thank you, Winston," Ella said with her hand on his face as he opened the back door. Winston said nothing but did have a small smirk as he looked upon both of us.

I patted him on the shoulder as we got into the back of the Rolls. He closed the door. He started the engine and we slowly moved East down 50th Street. From the window I remember Blake yelling as he came out of the church:

"Where the hell do you think you are going, Mickey? Where the hell are you going with my wife?"

"Too upset about the ring," I yelled, "getting her meds."

Blake stared. He knew Ella didn't take any meds. I could see Winston's pale blue eyes form the rear-view mirror. They squinted with appreciation.

It was unlike him, the polished, always smiling, never late Blake, but suddenly, without notice, he flipped me off. Ella rested her head on my shoulder.

As the car reached FDR Drive, I felt something underneath my buttocks. I reached down. I picked up the object. I held it up. It was Sophia's pricey Mont Blanc pen from the train to Boston. I put the pen next to mine in my jacket. I then peeked over to look at the newspaper that was on the passenger seat. Written on the crossword puzzle, in that characteristic all caps handwriting, was this:

BON

VOYAGE,

VIETNAM!

LOVE,

OTIS

We never went back to St. Patrick's Cathedral that day.

Sitting here, this 4th day of September 2018, in the same home where Ella had that summer party in 1968, I remember that July day in 1969 like it was this morning. I look at Ella sitting next to me and the pictures of our two kids, Jack and Aden. Ella rests her head on my shoulder. As I caress her gray hair while we look at the ocean in the distance, I say:

"I can't believe it all started with a stolen pen on that train ride to Boston."

She looks up at me and smiles as she says:

"Right, but it if weren't for a little tongue, we wouldn't be here right now."

The End